Doctor Right

S.L. Sterling

Doctor Right

ISBN: 978-1-989566-61-9

Paperback ISBN: 978-1-989566-62-6

Editor: Brandi Aquino, Editing Done Write

Cover Design: Thunderstruck Cover Design

Bella

January

"JUST SIGN HERE AND HERE." The stuffy lawyer who sat across from me pointed to the spots on the paper with the lid of his pen.

My stomach rolled as I looked over to Miles, who sat there with an impatient look on his face, waiting for me to sign us away forever. The constant ticking of the clock that stood in the corner was grating on my nerves. *Tick... tick... tick...*

I looked down at the forms in front of me, my hands beginning to sweat as I thought about what life was going to be like without him in my life.

"Miles, I—"

"Bella, just sign. Don't make this worse than the last few years. This part is simple and painless," he bit out.

I could feel the tears burning behind my eyes. "Miles, there has to be another way. Please, reconsider," I cried. "We could always look at adopting—"

"Bella, the time for options is up. You didn't want that and, unfortunately, I don't want this anymore," he said, waving his hand back and forth between us. "The last five years have taken a toll. I can't live another day of my life being miserable. It's time we just move on. We are over."

I looked across the desk at the emotionless face of the lawyer. *Tick... tick... tick...* It seemed even the clock was getting impatient with me. I wiped my hands on my jeans, picked up the pen, wiped the stray tear from my cheek that had fallen, and signed my name through blurry eyes.

I placed the pen down and reached for a tissue. The lawyer grabbed the papers and placed them in front of Miles. He nodded, picked up the pen, and confidently signed the paperwork, a hint of a smile on his face. He probably already had someone on the side, someone he could easily plant his seed in and produce the children he'd always wanted. Perhaps she already was pregnant. I'd never really know the truth and wasn't sure I wanted to.

After I walked out of that lawyer's office, I didn't look back. I went home to my small apartment and cried my eyes out one last time. Then I picked up all my broken pieces and focused on putting one foot in front of the other.

Three months later, I was right back where I was now —on the couch, crying my eyes out. My boss had laid me off.

* * *

May

THE FIRST FOUR months of being newly divorced was about uneventful as the first week we'd been married. However, the first week of being unemployed was hell. I'd spent countless hours looking for employment, and by Saturday night, I was burned out. I'd curled up on the couch in my pajamas and was watching an episode of my favourite show when my phone rang. I let out a sigh, debating not answering it. After eight, I knew it wouldn't be a job offer, so I glanced at the call display. It was the first time a smile had come to my lips all week.

"Brielle? Is it really you?" I cried into the receiver, happy to hear from my best friend.

"Bella! How are you, gorgeous?"

"I'm good. Just plugging along," I answered, turning the volume down on the TV.

"How's work?" she questioned.

I'd talked to Brielle over the past few months about

the divorce, but I'd yet to tell her about losing my job. It wasn't the way I wanted to start a conversation with her. I blew out a breath. "Well... it isn't. Cutbacks, you know," I said simply, trying hard not to allow the stress to creep up.

"Oh, Bella, I'm so sorry. How long?"

"I found out on Monday."

"God, I feel so bad now. I was going to call but figured you might need time to yourself to get over everything, and now I feel like I abandoned you."

"Don't be silly. You didn't abandon me."

"Yeah, but you needed me."

I grew quiet. I always needed Brielle. It had been hard since leaving Eastport. We'd been through so much together over the years. The fact that she wasn't right here had probably been the hardest part of going through this divorce. Not that Boston was that far. I'd headed back to Eastport right before we signed the divorce papers and spent a weekend. We'd had a great time, yet I felt bad adding extra work for her. She was busy running The Cooling Rack and looking after Emma. I didn't want to add my stresses to her day.

"Thanks. I always need you, but I needed some time, too. As for the new wrench in the gears, well, I'm just taking it day by day. Searching countless job websites for the same responses."

"Day by day is good. It's easier that way."

"So, to what do I owe this surprise?" I questioned, wanting to turn the attention off me.

Brielle was quiet for a moment. I could hear Emma in the background chattering away, then I heard Sawyer's deep voice answer her back. I was so happy for Brielle that she'd finally gotten back together with Sawyer.

"Brielle? Is everything okay?" I asked.

"Could be better. My assistant manager has left The Cooling Rack. She quit the day before yesterday."

"Oh, Brie, that is awful. I'm so sorry."

"Yes, especially with the baby on the way."

I could hear the panic in her voice. She'd found out she was pregnant again just last month. "Have you put out an ad to hire someone else?"

"I need someone I can trust. That's why I am calling you."

"Brie, I can't. I—"

"You told me yourself that you're looking for a way to start over. This would be it. Even if it's just for the summer. I mean, it would help you and me. Besides, you are the only one I know I can trust with my business, and you have great managerial experience."

She wasn't wrong. I was looking for a way to start over. I also had managerial experience, thanks to my last job promotion. I really didn't have an excuse, since I was now unemployed. Packing up and moving would not be that difficult.

"Well, when would you need me there?"

"Whenever you can be here for. Seriously, you do not know how much this would help me out. Plus, if you come now, you can get into the swing of things. If you don't want to stay or your boss calls you back, well, it will also give me time to find someone."

I had a small clue. I also knew how much it would truly help me put everything behind me. Perhaps a change of scenery was exactly what I needed, and the one thing I knew for sure was that my ex-husband wouldn't be back in Eastport because he was here, in Boston, with his newfound love. I could run into them anywhere. "Alright, let me organize some things and I will be there in the next couple of weeks."

"Oh, and no need to worry about a place. There are two condos available in the building we are in. Sawyer and I will get things started for you."

Brielle and I said our good-byes, and I hung up the phone and looked around my small one-bedroom apartment. I'd barely unpacked in the few months I'd lived here, almost as if I knew that something else would come along.

Asher

July

It had just stopped raining as I pulled up outside of The Cooling Rack. I cut the engine, unclipped my seatbelt, and stretched. It had been a long day. I'd had my meeting at Eastport General to see about office availability for what I'd hoped would become the home of my new private practice.

Afterward, I went to meet up with a doctor in the area who was looking at retiring. I already knew that a private practice was more my speed than hospital life. I'd spent my fair share in hospitals delivering babies, and I'd seen the shit that went on in ERs. I didn't want to get my hopes up, but I was excited about the idea of a new practice and a chance to start over.

I picked up the file folder containing all the details on the medical practice I was looking at buying. The doctor had been kind enough to put the file together and had given me at this meeting and headed inside the diner. I frequented the place in the last few weeks and loved it. At this time of the day, it was quieter, so it was a good place to sit down and go over these documents before contacting my lawyer, I thought to myself as I walked to the front door. However, when I stepped inside tonight, it surprised me to see that more than half the tables were still occupied.

After looking around, I spotted my usual table and made my way over. I'd just opened the folder and began looking over the notes I'd scribbled down when a menu was placed down in front of me. I looked up to be greeted by the same beautiful brunette that was normally here. The one I was certain I knew but still couldn't place.

She smiled. "Hello, welcome back to The Cooling Rack."

"Thanks," I replied, picking the menu up off the table. "What's the special today?" I questioned, looking over the menu to decide what it was I wanted for dinner tonight.

"Well, you look a little tired tonight, so I'm thinking

you need a cup of coffee, followed by the turkey club that's on special, and perhaps finish it with a couple of my favorite cookies—the double chocolate chip."

I smiled. Everything she'd suggested sounded wonderful. "That sounds great," I said, setting the menu off to the side, meeting her eyes. "I'm Asher." I held my hand out for her to take. "I figure it's time we formally introduce ourselves. After all, you can tell what I need to eat." Besides, I hoped that once I knew her name, I could place her.

"Bella. I'm the assistant manager here," she said, sliding her small hand into mine.

"Well, Bella, it's nice to meet you." I smiled, letting go of her soft hand.

"You too." She smiled and turned to walk away when suddenly it clicked.

"Bella, did you, by chance, go to Eastport High?" I questioned.

She nodded. "I did."

"You dated... Oh God, what was his name.... Miles Langdon, quarterback for the Eastport Lions."

"Yep, that would be me," she said, glancing over her shoulder as the jingle of the bell above the door rang out and two teenagers came in. "I'll be back with your order shortly." She grabbed the menu from the table and took off toward the kitchen.

I turned my attention back to the file in front of me and was soon deep into reading some of the information when a cup was quietly slid in front of me.

"Your coffee and cream." She held up a small basket full of creamers. "As always, there is sugar on the table."

"Thanks," I said, smiling. She'd learned how I liked my coffee the first time I'd had it and had never once forgotten, even when I hadn't seen her here for a few days. Most times, she'd even bring it over with the menu.

"So, did you play on the team with Miles?" she questioned.

"Yep, running back. We were always together."

"Oh my God, now I remember you. Asher Harrison, right?"

"That's me."

"You took me home the night after the huge win. The night Miles got super drunk." She giggled.

I remembered what a nightmare that night had been.

"I remember he was quite angry with you at the time for that." She smiled. "He'd gone on and on about wanting to hurt you. He thought you'd made a move."

The light blush across her cheeks caught my eyes, and I smiled. "Yep, he wasn't thrilled with me for that." I chuckled. "Him and I actually had a fight about in the locker room before the next game. The coach had to break it up." I chuckled.

"I know, I remember." She giggled. "I'll be back in a few minutes." She turned and made her way over to the table that had just left and began clearing it off. I tore my eyes away from her soft, curvy hips and went back to reading the file before me.

Shortly, a large plate was placed beside me, and I glanced over to see a large turkey club with a side of sweet potato fries in the center of the plate. "Thanks," I mumbled, placing the documents aside.

"Those look important." She glanced to the thick stack of papers while placing a set of silverware on the table.

"Somewhat..." I shrugged. "Just some business documents. Looks like the place kind of cleared out," I said, looking around the diner. Only one table on the opposite side of the room was now full.

"Normally does. Our next busy time is coming up though, close to seven, right as the doctors start their break at the hospital."

"I was going to ask what time you closed. I didn't want to be holding you up from something more important just because I need to eat. No reason I couldn't take this to-go."

"We close at nine. You have lots of time. I'm normally here until ten." She softly smiled. "You're welcome to stay as long as you need."

"Care to sit down and join me?" I questioned. "You must have a break coming up or something."

"I do, but I couldn't." She glanced around to, I assumed, see what she had left to do. "I just normally work through my break at night."

"That's not a good practice. Take a seat," I said, nodding to the empty bench across the way. "We're practically friends, having gone to the same high school." She slowly sat down, looking around as if someone might see her. "So, you work here long?"

"About a month and a half now."

"And you, are you from around here? Wait, of course you are. That was a silly thing to ask."

I shook my head. "Not anymore. I moved away for school. Then, you know, life happened. I'm just renting a small place here for now. There are some things I need to sort out in my personal life and my work life. Once I've got those things figured out, I'll decide where it is I'll end up."

"Well, you chose a good place to figure things out in. Eastport has always been great for clearing one's mind," she said, smiling. "You know, in case you forgot."

"Ah, so you're still a local?"

"No, Miles and I, we moved to Boston after college. He got a job, and we got married. I've just came back to help a dear friend of mine and to do some soul searching of my own."

I nodded, shoving a fry into my mouth. "Seems like we are both on the same sort of path. How is Miles? Is he here with you? It would be great to catch up. We lost touch after high school."

Bella glanced over at me and slowly shook her head. "I wouldn't know how he is. We divorced seven months ago."

"Oh, I'm sorry to hear that."

"Don't be, I'm not."

The bell rang out above the door again as someone came in, and she jumped, looking over her shoulder. "I've got to go. Enjoy your dinner."

Once she was gone, I turned my attention to my dinner. Occasionally, I'd look over at her and watch as she dealt with one customer after another. When my plate was clear, I shoved it to the side and turned my attention back to the pile of documents, reading over the contract this doctor had drawn up.

Reaching the last page of the contract, everything looked good, but I'd still needed to have my lawyer check it over before I signed. I was just about to send him an email requesting a meeting when Bella appeared at the side of my table.

"Would you like your desert now with another coffee?" I heard her soft voice ask.

I looked up and met those gorgeous dark eyes and nodded. "Only if you'll join me," I said, winking.

She softly smiled and shook her head. "I'd love to, but I'm the only one here tonight. It's going to get busy."

I couldn't get over how much I loved that soft-pink hue on her cheeks. She was attractive in high school, and had Miles not gotten to her first, I'd have gone after her, but now there was something even more attractive about her. I wanted to get to know better. "Well, that is a problem," I said.

"It is?" she questioned, looking around.

"Yes, well, I love desert, but I hate eating it alone." There was that blush again.

"Oh, that is a problem." She giggled. "How do you suggest we solve it?"

"Well, I was thinking, perhaps we could share a dessert later, after your shift is over," I replied, meeting her eyes. It wasn't like me to be this forward.

"Oh, I don't know." I watched her throat as she swallowed hard. She began fidgeting with the watch on her wrist as she stood there. "I'm really not looking for—"

"Just as friends. I'm not looking for anything either." I winked, trying to make her feel a little more comfortable at my suggestion and not think I was some creep.

She thought for a minute, then smiled. "All right, I guess... we could do that," she said, playing with the thin gold chain around her neck.

"Okay then. I'll be right here." I pulled my phone from my coat pocket, getting ready to email my lawyer.

"I'll sit here until you kick me out, then I will wait for you in the parking lot." I winked.

She nodded, smiled, and turned away from me. Occasionally, I'd notice she was looking over my way, a soft smile on her lips as she served the rest of the customers through the evening.

Bella

I'D JUST LOCKED up the back door after letting all the staff out and went back out to the front to exit from the front door. I looked out the front window and could see Asher sitting in his car. Reaching into the display case, I pulled the last four double chocolate chip cookies and placed them into a bag, then I poured the last of the coffee into two paper cups, placing a lid on both. I shut the lights off, except for the ones behind the counter, and carried everything over to the door. I carefully punched the code into the alarm and then unlocked the front door, slipping outside.

Asher met me on the sidewalk, grabbing the bag and coffee from my hands so I could take my keys and lock the door. Together we walked to his car, where he opened the passenger side door for me and handed me the coffee and cookies. Then he ran around the front of the car and climbed in.

"I noticed you don't have a car here?" he said, glancing at the empty parking lot.

I shook my head. "It's nice weather. I prefer to walk. Besides, I'm near to here."

"I see, even this late at night you walk?" he questioned. "Don't you worry about safety?"

"Yep, and yep, but it's a pretty safe neighbourhood."

"So, where shall we go?"

I shrugged. "I don't know."

"Well, we could go to the park, or to the waterfront, but if there is another low-key place you like to hang out at, say the word. We'll go wherever you want."

For a moment, I thought about it. I'd been back in Eastport for two months, and the only places I'd visited were The Cooling Rack, my condo, the grocery store, and Brielle and Sawyer's. On my day off, I hadn't walked through the park or the waterfront. I let out a breath and thought for a moment.

"I guess we could go to Eastport Park." I smiled, pulling out two cookies and handing one to Asher.

"The park it is." He grabbed the cookie from me, shoving it into his mouth, and put the car into reverse.

A little while later, we were both walking barefoot in

the sand, side by side. We sipped on our coffee as we walked.

"So how long have you been in Eastport?" I asked.

"Hmmm, almost a month," Asher replied, chuckling. "It's sort of what the doctor ordered."

I frowned. "Doctor?" Was he sick?

"Yeah, I just got out of a pretty nasty relationship and needed to get myself back on my path, clear my head, and take control of things again."

I looked out over the water, my own memories of divorce flooding my mind. "Those are the same things that brought me here to Eastport as well. That and the fact that I'd lost my job, and my best friend needed a manager to help at The Cooling Rack."

"So you too, huh? Was it a nasty divorce?"

"Are there other kinds?" I replied, looking out over the water.

"I guess not. How long were you guys married?"

"Five years. Seemed as soon as we signed our marriage certificate the troubles began."

"Any kids?" he questioned.

Sadness flooded me. That question would haunt me for the rest of my life. I swallowed hard, smiled, and shook my head. Somehow, I needed to be okay with never being able to have children, and I would have been, but Miles had made me feel so damn awful about it, it had made it harder to accept. "No, none."

"Well, that is probably better. It could have made things really bad."

"Oh, it did. Even not having them."

"What do you mean?"

"That's why we got divorced. Miles wanted them so bad and…"

"And you didn't?" Asher said, slowly walking forward.

I said nothing. I didn't want to rehash the entire experience. Instead, I cleared my throat, took a sip of my coffee, and asked, "It wasn't that simple. What about you?"

"No, no kids."

We both grew quiet, then almost as if we were both thinking the same thing, we stopped walking and looked at one another.

"Just to reiterate, I'm not looking for anything long term," we said in unison.

We laughed. Everything felt lighter. It was if someone had lifted a weight off both our chests. We began laughing again as we looked at one another. I looked down to the ground as Asher cleared his throat. "Well, now that we have gotten that out of the way…"

"Yeah." I softly smiled at him.

"Care to continue our walk?"

I didn't answer. Instead, I just nodded, and we began walking, sipping the last of our coffees and eating the last of our cookies, until we'd circled back to the car. He opened my door for me and waited while I climbed into the front seat, and then he made his way around to the driver's side.

"Bella, not to rehash the subject, but I just want you to know I'm just looking for a friend, someone to hang out with, to pass the time with. The last few months have been hard on me, most of my friends sided with her, so it's like I'm starting all over again." he said, firing up the engine.

It was as if he had read my mind. "I'd like that," I replied.

"Good, me too," he said, placing his large, warm hand on mine.

Asher was a good-looking man, and from what I remembered, he'd been good-looking in high school too. As we drove, I studied his chiseled features, perhaps a little too long and hard for someone who wasn't looking for anything more than friendship. He finally pulled into the parking lot of The Cooling Rack and turned to look at me.

"If you'd like, I'll take you home, or I can leave you here, so you can walk. I don't want to push you to give me your address."

I thought for a moment, glancing down. It was a little late, even though this part of the neighbourhood was safe. "You can take me home. You seem like a trustworthy guy." I winked. "I just live over on Eastport Park Drive."

"It's amazing how you forget an area you once knew

so well," Asher said as he plugged the address into his GPS and followed the directions and turned onto my street, which from there I gave him directions to the condo. He pulled up in front of the big white building and put the car in park.

"There you go, Bella," he said, his large hand resting on the gearshift. "Safe and sound. I hope you had a good time."

"Thank you. I did. Will I see you sometime soon?"

"I think you might." He winked. "I'm sort of addicted to the coffee at The Cooling Rack." He chuckled.

I smiled. "Until next time then." And with that, I got out of the car and walked to the main door, glancing over my shoulder many times to see Asher still sitting in his car at the end of the walkway, waiting and watching to make sure I got inside.

One Week Later

IT HAD BEEN one week since the night Asher and I had gone out after work. Part of me was upset that I hadn't attempted to exchange phone numbers. He'd seemed like a nice guy, and I was excited to have hopefully made another friend, aside from Brielle and Sawyer. Yet I still hadn't mentioned a word about that night, or about Asher, to Brielle.

I let out a sigh and finished placing our order for our supplies when Brielle walked into the office.

"Bella, what are you doing on Sunday?" she questioned.

"Hmmm, let me check my calendar... Oh wait, that's right, no plans!" I laughed.

"Sawyer and I would like to have you for dinner on Sunday."

I shrugged. If I knew Brielle, this was another attempt at unsuccessfully matching me with yet another doctor from Sawyer's work. "No, wait, I have to work. Did you forget?"

"Of course not, silly. You'll finish before dinner," she said, making a silly face at me. "I'm the boss, remember!" She laughed, flinging her purse onto the desk and flopping into the chair in the corner. "I'll just schedule someone else to close."

She was being too accommodating just for me to come and have dinner with them. Something was up. I looked over at Brielle. "Uh-huh, who am I meeting this week?" I asked, letting out a deep sigh.

"Okay...okay. If you must know, he is a cardiologist. Very good-looking, highly successful, and very single," Brielle replied, smiling at me with excitement.

"Brielle, please, I am not ready for a relationship. I don't know how many more times I need to say it. I said it after the brain surgeon, after the psychiatrist, and after the endocrinologist you guys thought would be perfect for me."

"I know, you keep saying that. You just need to be open to the possibilities of a new relationship. We just want to see you happy."

"I am happy. Thrilled. I'd be even happier if you'd stop trying to fix me up with every single guy you know. I am happy just focusing on this job, and I've been focusing on decorating my place and committing to my yoga practice. For once, I'm focusing on me, and it feels fantastic."

"I agree. You have been doing all those things, but you need some spice in your life too," she said, pulling up a chair and sitting down beside me.

I let out a breath and looked at my best friend. "Spice can come when I'm ready for it. Honestly, I just want to focus on me. It's what I desperately need right now, Brie. Before I let someone else in, I need to focus on myself and get my life in order." I was practically begging my best friend to stop trying to set me up with people. I needed to just focus on the things that were important to me. It was something I'd never done before.

Just then a knock came to the door, and we both looked over to see Tomi, one of the staff, leaning against the doorframe. "Sorry to interrupt, but, Bella, someone is here to see you."

"Did they say who it was?"

Tomi smiled. "It's a guy, says that you'll know who it is." She smiled.

Brielle looked at me with surprise on her face. "Well, well, keeping something from your best friend, are you?" She laughed, getting all giddy with excitement, grabbing me and shaking me. "You little liar." She laughed again.

"My God, Brie, I'm not keeping anything from you at all. Now, if you'll calm down and excuse me..." I said, getting up.

"Not a chance. No way are you keeping this from me," she said, getting up and following me through the kitchen.

I glanced through the hole in the door to see Asher standing off to the side, hands in his pockets. He couldn't have appeared at a worse time I thought to myself. He was wearing perfectly fitted jeans and a white ribbed-knit sweater that hugged him in all the right spots. He looked amazing. I licked my lips and then glanced at Brielle and gave her the same look she'd shared with me so many times over the years.

"Uh-huh. Not hiding anything hmmm..." Brielle giggled.

"I'm not," I replied.

"Okay, okay, fine. Go." She laughed.

I pushed the door open and stepped out behind the counter just as Asher turned around.

"Hey," I whispered, making my way over to him.

"Hey. I was hoping you'd be here. I had to go out of town for a few days, but I wanted to stop in and see you before I made my way home. I was hoping you might like to go out for dinner sometime this week."

I bit my bottom lip while thinking of any reason I could to get out of dinner. I even went to the extent of pulling my phone out of my back pocket and scrolling through my very empty, non-existent social calendar while my mind raced with any reason I couldn't go.

"It's not a date, if that is what you are thinking." He'd read my mind. He cleared his throat and placed his hand on my arm, pulling me aside. "Listen, I could really use a night out to take my mind off of some things, and since you are the only person I know here, I thought I'd ask you."

I met his eyes and could see the look of someone who really needed a friend. "Sure, what night?"

"Tomorrow?"

"Tomorrow works," I said. "What time?"

"How about I pick you up at seven?"

I thought for a moment, and then nodded. "Seven it is."

"Great." He rubbed his hands together and smiled.

"Oh, do you like seafood? I've had a craving for it since I came to Eastport."

I nodded. "Love it."

"Okay, I'll see you tomorrow night."

Asher didn't give me a minute to protest or change my mind because he was already in his car and heading out of the parking lot by the time I realized what it was I'd just agreed to. As I shoved my phone back into my pants pocket, I realized I couldn't even text him to cancel because, once again, I hadn't gotten his number. *I really needed to get his number.*

I let out a sigh and made my way back to the office. The kitchen door had just swung shut behind me when I heard Brielle.

"Well? What was that all about?" she grilled as I walked through the door and back to our shared office.

"Nothing, just a friendly conversation."

Brielle stood there, a knowing look on her face. "Whatever, not with a hottie like that. I can guarantee it wasn't just a friendly conversation. Are you seeing him?"

I shook my head and laughed. "Brielle, not being ready for a relationship isn't just an answer I give you to stop fixing me up with people. It was also the answer I gave him. He's just a friend," I said.

"A friend?" Brielle was quiet for a moment. Then she looked at me. "Please, Bella, don't disappoint me."

"Yes, he's a friend. If you must know, we went to high

school together. He was actually one of guys who played on the high school football team with Miles."

"Oh." I could hear the disappointment in her voice as she flopped back down into her chair.

"Yes, oh." I giggled, turning my attention back to what I'd been working on.

Asher

I JUST HUNG up the phone after confirming reservations for two at The Harbourview Restaurant and returned to the bathroom where I started the shower. I'd just finished my workout for the day, and I had a little less than two hours to get ready before I picked up Bella.

I quickly showered, dried, and then wrapped the white towel around my waist. I shaved, then splashed some cologne on my neck. Then I wandered over to the closet, sifting through the hanging clothes, until I found my favorite pair of dark-blue jeans and crew neck.

I glanced at my reflection in the mirror before grabbing my jacket off the back of the chair. I made my way to my car and sped off toward the local flower shop.

I felt it was necessary to take her flowers; I had told

myself many times in my head this wasn't a date, but my mother had taught me early in life that women like flowers, so I'd grabbed a bouquet of light-pink carnations, the same colour her cheeks went as she blushed. Armed with flowers, I pulled up outside of her building.

As I sat there waiting for her to come down, I kept looking to the bouquet. I was about to get out and dump them in the garbage bin when I saw her step out of the building. I could barely take my eyes off her. She walked toward the car, dressed in snug-fitting jeans and a light-pink sweater under a beige jacket. Her dark hair was wavy and soft and bounced lightly at her shoulders as she walked. I quickly got out of the of the car and walked around to her side, the flowers behind my back.

"You look great," I said, not wanting to come on too strong, but not wanting her to think I hadn't noticed.

"Thank you, as do you," she said, smiling at me.

I opened the passenger's side door and waited while she climbed into the car, then I handed her the bouquet. "For you."

"Oh..." she said with a look of surprise. "They're, um... they're beautiful," she said, seeming confused.

"Yeah, after I bought them, I wondered why I had. See, it's just my mother always told me that girls like flowers, and well...you are a girl," I explained, nerves fluttering through me.

"I am and I do," she said, smiling, bringing the flowers to her nose to smell them. "Thank you, they are beautiful. They are also very unexpected, but beautiful," she said, glancing up at me.

I swallowed hard, shut the door, and made my way around to the driver's side door, taking a deep breath before I climbed back into the car. "Hope you're hungry."

"I am. Where are we headed?"

"Well, I thought we'd go to The Harbourview."

"Oh. Okay," she said, looking out the window and not meeting my gaze.

I glanced over. I could tell she was uncomfortable. Was it me, the flowers, had I overstepped the 'friends' thing? "Is something wrong with that restaurant? I just looked up 'local seafood restaurant' on the computer, so if it's no good, I'd rather know now. Nothing worse than horrible seafood."

She shook her head, but I still wasn't convinced. "No, it's nothing. The Harbourview has got fantastic food."

"Then what is it, because that's not a face of someone who likes food in a restaurant and is happy to be going to it."

She shifted uncomfortably in her seat and looked over at me. "Really, it's nothing, really. The flowers are really pretty. Thank you," she said, pulling her seat belt across her.

I wasn't sure I believed her, but I'd also learned from my previous relationship that dwelling on things wasn't healthy, nor was it smart. It was a surefire way to end up in an argument, even with a friend. Instead, I pulled away from the curb and headed toward the restaurant's, determined to make this a night of fun for both of us.

"So, what is your choice?" I questioned, looking over the menu just as our drinks arrived at the table.

"Hmm, I thought that the Lobster Bisque looks good, but then, so does the Lobster Tagliatelle. What about you?"

"Funny, I was looking at the Tagliatelle or the Grilled Atlantic Salmon."

"Oh, I missed the salmon," she said, smiling over at me then looking back down at her menu as she picked up her wine and took a sip.

"So, what are you doing to heal yourself?" I questioned. "You told me you were focusing on that."

"Well, aside from working, I have been putting a lot of focus on me. I have been setting up my new place, spending time with Brielle, my best friend, and her husband, Sawyer, and Emma, their little girl. I've been doing yoga, and recently I started a meditation group at the yoga studio. Honestly, I'm focusing on me and the things I want to do. I didn't get to do many of those things while I was married."

"That's good. How are you liking meditation?"

"Um, well, I have done it twice, and honestly, I'm not sure I get it. Silencing the mind isn't as easy as one would think, but I'm trying. I find I get a lot out of yoga, more so than in meditation."

"Yoga is fantastic! I actually used to practice at a local studio before I moved here. It was always what I needed to clear my mind after a tough day."

"What about you?" she asked, sipping her wine again.

"The same as you. Just focusing on myself. I took some time off from work to clear my head, and I've started running again and hitting the gym. There is something very healing about running on the beach in the early morning, watching the sunrise. Have you ever tried it?" I smiled, passing the bread basket that had been placed on our table.

"Thank you," she said, reaching in and grabbing a piece and placing it on the small bread plate beside her. "I used to run in high school but stopped when I went to college, then got married, and it was just another thing I allowed my life to take over."

"I understand. Well, perhaps you could join me sometime?"

"I'll think about it." She picked up her bread and tore

a little piece off, shoving it into her mouth and looking around like she was trying to avoid being seen.

"So, I couldn't help but notice you looked a little upset in the car. This wasn't a terrible choice, was it?"

She looked over at me, then shook her head. "No, not at all. I've heard the food is fantastic here."

"Bella? Bella, is that you?" a woman's voice called out.

I looked in the direction the voice came from, and suddenly a woman appeared. "Bella, it is you!"

"Oh, hey," she said unenthusiastically before glancing over at me.

"How are things? I hope you're okay? God, I could kill my brother for what he did to you," the woman said as she stood at the side of our table, giving me the occasional glance.

"Yeah, well, it's over now. I'm fine."

I could see the tension in her shoulders as the woman looked between her and me and then back to her as if questioning what it was she was doing here with me. The conversation had literally stalled, so I jumped in.

"Hi, I'm Asher, a good friend of Bella's," I said, shoving my hand out toward this woman.

"Hi. Stacey. So, you say you're a good friend of Bella's?" she said, glancing my way. "Perhaps I'm not so angry with my brother after all. Perhaps I should be angry at you, Bella, for cheating on my brother. Anyway, I'll talk to you later," she said, taking off in the direction she came.

Bella smiled at me uncomfortably and shrugged. "That was Mile's sister. She works here and apparently, she hasn't changed one bit. She used to spread rumors about me in highschool, and she apparently going to do the same now."

"Why didn't you say something? We could have gone somewhere else!"

"I didn't want to do that. I hoped she wasn't working tonight, and at first, I thought I was safe, but then I caught sight of her. She has a hard time minding her own business, as you can see. Plus, all that talk about how she hates her brother for what he did to me is a lie. However, now it looks like she'll have a real hate on for me," Bella said, taking another bite of her bread.

"Don't worry about it. People love to talk. It says way more about them than it does about you." I winked. I'd learned that over the past six months as rumours flew around about me.

Bella smiled at me. "Yeah, and she loves to start them. I can almost hear her now."

"So, let her. I used to tell people when they'd approach me with the latest rumour they'd heard to add to that rumour whatever the hell they wanted. That would just make them stand and stare at me, wondering if I were serious." I chuckled.

"I bet. So, you had someone like that in your life too, then?"

"Oh, try about ten of them. All my ex's friends. I do not know what she told them, but the things I heard just blew my mind."

Bella let out a little giggle. "I'm sorry that happened to you."

"And I am sorry I chose the restaurant your sister-in-law worked at."

Dinner finally came, and the rest of the meal passed, drinks flowed, and so did conversation. We avoided our past issues as a topic of discussion and talked about our hobbies and things we were interested in. Turned out we had more than a few things in common, and before we knew it, we had an entire list of events and things to do throughout the summer. When the server set the bill down on the edge of the table, we both reached for it, but I grabbed it first.

"Asher, please, let me see it."

I opened the billfold and shook my head. "No, I got it," I said, pulling out my credit card, placing it on top of the bill.

"No, that isn't fair. I'd like to pay my share."

Asher looked at me and smiled. "How about you get it next time?" I said, winking at her.

I was surprised she didn't fight me. Instead, she just agreed. As soon as I paid the bill, we walked out of the restaurant together and climbed into my car.

"Thank you," I said, before starting the engine.

"For?"

"For joining me, taking my mind off of things, and for being my friend."

"You are welcome," she replied. "And thank you for dinner and for teaching me to learn that it's okay to let people talk." She giggled, placing her hand on top of mine. "It means a lot," she said in a hushed whisper.

"You're welcome."

Our eyes locked and silence fell between us. We sat there staring at one another, neither saying a word. I could have gotten lost in her eyes if I allowed myself, but I finally tore mine away from hers and cleared my throat. "We should exchange numbers. Maybe I can convince you to come for a run with me one day this week," I said, reaching into my pocket to pull out my phone.

She reached into her purse, pulling her phone from inside, and smiled. "I think that is a good idea, and perhaps I could convince you to come and join me for some yoga."

"No convincing needed. I'll be there. Just let me know when," I said.

We switched phones and entered our own information into the contacts area and switched back, then I started the engine and drove to her condo. We said our good-byes, and I waited while she walked up to the door. Once she was inside, I was about to pull away from the curb when my phone vibrated to let me know I had a message. I reached for it, looking at the screen to see Bella had already sent a message. I clicked it open and read it.

> BELLA: Thank you for a wonderful evening. Looking forward to the next ;)

I smiled. I had a feeling this was the beginning of a wonderful new friendship.

Bella

One week Later

I DROPPED my yoga mat inside the door and kicked off my sneakers. I'd taken a yoga class down in the park this morning. It had been a gorgeous day, and yoga had become my favorite way to spend a Saturday morning. I went into the kitchen and turned the kettle on, looking forward to my cup of chamomile tea, when the phone rang.

"Hello," I said, without checking my caller ID.

"Bella, it's Miles."

Irritated, I made a mental note to make sure next time I checked to see who was calling before answering. "What do you need?" I asked, feeling the irritation climb into my body.

"I've got some mail for you here at the house. Thought I'd let you know and find out where to send it."

I knew Sawyer was going on a medical retreat next week and had asked him to stop and pick up some things I'd left behind. "I'll have Sawyer pick them up when he is in town next week, okay?"

"Okay then. I also heard from my sister. She said she saw you the other night with some guy? What's going on?"

I remembered Asher's words from that night. *People will talk; let them. It says more about them than it does you.* No matter how true those words may have been, it still didn't stop me from being bothered.

"She said it appeared you were on a date."

I softly smiled to myself. "Of course, it did."

"Is it true?"

"Miles, it will be whatever your sister said it was."

"Bella, what is that supposed to mean?" I could hear the irritation line his voice.

"Exactly what I said. My word certainly will change no one's mind. Never did. However, I wanted to let you know Asher says hello."

The line was quiet for a moment. "Asher? As in Asher Harrison?" he asked, his voice cracking like he was still going through puberty. "You were on a date with Asher Harrison?"

"Yes. Now, I have to go. I will give Sawyer your address." I didn't wait for a good-bye. Instead, I hung up. I did not know what had possessed me to lie to Miles, telling him it was Asher I had been out with. It certainly wasn't to make him jealous, or perhaps it was. Perhaps I'd done it to give him a taste of his own medicine after the five years of abuse I'd dealt with. It felt good to kind of stick something to him. Either way, I went back to making my tea and started cutting up some cucumber for a light snack.

I'd just sat down when I heard a knock at the door. I was on my way to answer it when I heard a familiar voice call out, "Come on, woman, open up."

I laughed and opened the door. "Come on in." I giggled. "Want a tea?" I questioned, looking at a frazzled Brielle.

"Oh, yes, please. I have an hour to myself. Sawyer and Emma are napping."

I closed the door and went to the kitchen, pouring Brielle a tea and carried it into the living room, placing it in front of her.

"Thanks. It's been a long morning," she said, releasing a yawn. Her hair was everywhere, and she looked exhausted, quite a difference from how she appeared at work every day.

"Of course. Oh, before I forget, can Sawyer pop by Miles' place and get some mail of mine and a few other things that he has of mine next week before he returns from his conference?"

"Sure, I'll let him know. So, tell me, how was dinner the other night?"

I'd made the mistake of asking Brielle to help me get ready for dinner the other night with Asher. She had been good about it, until she wanted to look at my old yearbooks to see what he had looked like then. I'd dug them out of a bin in the closet, and while I was busy getting ready, she'd flipped through the pages, glancing at images of a young Asher. I figured the first chance she would have, she would ask me all about it, and I was right.

"It was nice. We had dinner at The Harbourview. Although I ran into Stacey. Of course, she had to stuff her nose into everything. Plus, she told Miles. I'm not sure if he called just now to tell me about the mail or to find out if what she had told him was true."

"What did you say?"

I giggled. "I told him Asher said hello."

"You didn't."

"Yep, I did. Just thought I'd try to give him a taste of what my last five years were like, although I doubt it affected him any. Although, I know there were times in highschool that he thought Asher was trying to steal me from him. Oh and I heard through the grapevine that his new girlfriend is pregnant, and they are planning their wedding."

"Oh God, already? Did he even give himself a chance to get over you?" Brielle questioned.

"He was over me before he'd even contacted a lawyer. I'm sure of that. It's honestly not an enormous surprise."

"Guess I should tell you that Sheila was in the diner the other day, too," Brielle replied.

"What for? She never comes in there."

"Oh, she told me she was meeting a friend there. However, no one showed up, and after an hour, she left. I'm guessing she was there to see you, or perhaps see if Asher and you showed up together."

Didn't she have anything better to do with her time? I rolled my eyes and giggled.

"Apparently not. Knowing Miles, he put her up to it. Now he knows the truth, or part of the truth." I giggled.

"Anyway, enough about those two! When are you seeing Mr. Gorgeous again?" Brielle questioned.

I rolled my eyes at my friend and sighed. "Look, we are just friends, nothing more. Now please, stop with that. He is good-looking, but honestly, Brie, I'm not looking for anything."

"You say that a lot," Brielle cried, letting out a sigh. "The least you could do is humour me. Honestly. Make up something," she said, laughing.

I picked up my tea and took a sip, then looked to my best friend and started laughing. "You are so impossible."

Just then, my phone vibrated against the table. Brielle

leaned forward in time to see Asher's name flash on the screen. She looked at me and lifted her eyebrows.

"Just friends, huh? Does he know that?"

I knew Brielle was just trying to get under my skin, and it was working. "I really like Asher, and if things were different..." I could feel my cheeks heating at my realization.

"If things were different... what?" Brielle said, sitting forward on the couch, waiting for me to continue.

I let out a sigh. "Well, perhaps if things were different, I'd consider dating him." I shrugged.

Brielle looked at me, a mischievous smile on her face. "What?"

"How do we get you ready?" She giggled. "He may be just too good for you to pass up."

Just then, a knock came to the door. I shook my head and got up. I opened the door to see a dishevelled Sawyer standing there holding a crying Emma. "Bella, please tell me Brie is here."

"Yes, come on in."

"What's wrong?" she called from the living room.

"I have to go to work. There's an emergency, and they've called me in," Sawyer said, handing Emma over to me. I watched as he made his way over to Brielle, bent down, and gave her a kiss good-bye, then he made his way over to me again and kissed Emma, then kissed me on the cheek.

"Guess we are on our own for dinner, eh, Emma," Brielle said as I placed Emma on her lap.

"You guys can always have dinner with me tonight," I said, thinking about what I could make that was easy.

"Sounds perfect," Brie said as she bounced Emma on her lap making her laugh.

———

BRIELLE AND EMMA left shortly after nine. After taking a hot bath, I crawled into bed. I'd just begun reading the book I was in the middle of when my phone vibrated against my nightstand. I reached for the phone and smiled when I saw Asher's name on my screen.

ASHER: Ignoring me, are you?

BELLA: Depends, who's spreading rumours now lol

ASHER: Me ;P

I couldn't help but laugh.

ASHER: What are you doing?

I quickly snapped a picture of my book on top of my flannel-clad legs and sent it off.

ASHER: Ohhh baby. Stop sending
dirty pictures.

BELLA: :O You wish!

ASHER: How did you guess ;)

I rolled my eyes and laughed.

ASHER: What are you doing
tomorrow?

I glanced to my calendar. Again, it was empty. I really needed to fill it up. I couldn't even use work as an excuse since Brielle had given me a week off since I'd need to cover for her for two weeks later in the summer.

BELLA: Not a lot, see it's empty :(

I quickly attached a screenshot of my calendar for him to see. I waited as those three dots appeared bouncing around excitedly.

ASHER: Fear not! Meet me at the
beach for 8.

BELLA: Eight! In the morning?

ASHER: Yep, 8 in the morning. We'll go for a run then have breakfast afterward, then we will head off to an antique market I found up the coast.

I smiled as I read his message. It sounded like a lovely day, and part of me was excited, but the other part was hesitant.

ASHER: Don't overthink it. Just say you'll join me.

I tapped the screen of my phone while biting my lip, trying to decide if I should say yes or no. I was afraid that perhaps I'd been giving him the wrong signals. God, I hoped I wasn't.

ASHER: You're overthinking

BELLA: No I'm not!

ASHER: Then what is taking you so long?

BELLA: You're impossible! I'll see you at 8 ;)

ASHER: ;) I look forward to it.

Asher

I'D LISTENED to her laugh all day long, and I still wasn't tired of hearing that sound. We approached the door to her condo, and she dug around in her purse, looking for the keys as the smell of pizza drove us crazy.

"I'm starving. That smells so good, and I... seriously... why can't I find my keys?" she cried, now furiously digging deeper into her purse.

"Well, we could always just park ourselves on the floor here and eat the pizza!" I said, glancing around as the smell of pepperoni made my mouth water.

She let out a laugh and shook her head. "You're ridiculous! Actually, look, we're saved from hallway pizza!" she said, pulling her keys from her purse and holding them in the air.

I chuckled as I followed her into her condo. "Go on

in. We can eat in the living room. I'll just grab some plates and glasses."

I carried the pizza into the living room and set the box down on the small coffee table in front of the couch. Her place was beautifully decorated, and I smiled as I glanced at the small bookshelf in the corner. I took a quick glance at some titles and noticed we both had many of Wayne Dyer's books. He had become one of my favourites since my relationship took a dive. I then turned my attention to the floor-to-ceiling window and wandered over to see that her place looked out over the water. There was even a small bistro table and chairs on the balcony.

"We could always eat out on the balcony," I suggested, just as Bella stepped into the living room. "Watch the sunset."

"Whatever you would like. I figured you'd just like to relax and watch Netflix or something."

"Well, I'm shocked," I said, trying hard to hide the smile on my lips.

"Why? What's wrong? Did they get our order wrong?"

"No, but I wonder, are you suggesting that we... Netflix and chill?" I said, still trying not to laugh.

I watched as her cheeks went to my favourite shade of pink and a smile came to her lips. "Oh God... I did, didn't I," she said, burying her face into her hands.

"You did." I smiled, walking over to her.

She stepped into me and buried her face into my chest, wrapping her arms around my waist as she laughed. "My God, I can't believe what I did."

Instinctively, I wrapped my arms around her, hugging her close to me. She smelled heavenly, and we stood there, her holding me and me holding her.

The day had gone so smoothly. Better than I had thought it would. We'd gone on our run, then headed to a small breakfast diner. We drove up the coast, listening to music, and had spent the day walking through the large antique market I'd found online. The pizza and a movie were an impromptu suggested by her.

I felt her arms slowly slide from my waist, and so I too let her go. She took a seat on the edge of the couch and flipped open the pizza box. She held out a plate to me, which I took and sat down next to her.

"We can eat outside if you'd like," she said, pulling a slice of pizza from the box and placing it on her plate.

I shook my head, leaning back on the couch. It had been a long day. We'd had a lot of sun and fresh air and no doubt she was as tired as I. "Nah, let's kick back, relax, find a movie."

She smiled and leaned back against the couch, taking a bite of her pizza. "Sounds like a good idea."

Two hours later, she was curled into my side, a blanket over her legs as we watched a movie. She'd chosen a thriller, and from the looks of things, it hadn't been a wise choice. She seemed petrified.

"Oh God... why do I watch these?" she cried as she snuggled closer to me and hid her eyes behind her fingers.

I couldn't help but chuckle. She was so damn cute. "It's not that bad," I said, putting my arm around her and pulling her close to me.

"It is! And why are you laughing at me?" she questioned, gripping my shirt.

"I'm not laughing at you," I said, grabbing her side causing her to laugh. "Okay, perhaps I'm laughing at you."

"Oh God, don't do that. I'm so ticklish," she said, grabbing my hand.

"Oh... are you now?" I grabbed her side once again as she laughed hard, forgetting about the movie.

"Yes, please...stop..." she said, laughing hard as I continued tickling her.

She grabbed my hand. "Please, Asher," she pleaded, out of breath, continuing to laugh, "Please, stop."

"Okay... okay..." I said, holding my hands up as if I were innocent. I pulled her into me. "Now, behave yourself. Let's watch the rest of the movie."

WHEN THE CREDITS ROLLED, I felt Bella stretch. I rubbed her arm just as she sat up. She let out a yawn and stretched again.

"Did you fall asleep?" I questioned, stretching myself.

"Perhaps." She smiled, grabbing our plates and glasses, then heading toward the kitchen. "You are very warm, and I was very comfortable."

"I see. I'm warm and comfortable?"

I followed her to the kitchen and stood in the doorway, watching as she slipped everything into her dishwasher.

"You are." She shrugged and giggled, turning to me and wrapping herself around me again.

I really liked this girl, and I knew I needed to get out of here before I made a mistake and kissed her. Her lips had been on my mind all night, and I'd almost kissed her once before while tickling her. "Well, I should get going," I said, glancing at my watch to see that it was almost midnight.

She nodded. "I guess morning does come early."

I turned and made my way to the door, sliding on my shoes. I wished I wasn't in the position I was, just having had my heart broken. I wished I'd met her under better circumstances and that I was ready to move forward into another relationship. Only when I looked over to see her standing against the wall, watching me, I was sure I saw a hint of want in her eyes.

"Thank you for today and tonight."

"Of course," I said, making my way over to her and placing my hand against the wall above her head. "I had a wonderful time." I looked down into her eyes, brushing a strand of hair out of the way.

She looked up at me. "Call me?" she questioned. "I'm off this week."

God, it didn't matter how much I knew I shouldn't kiss her, how much I wasn't ready. All I could think about was what her lips would feel like against mine. This wasn't the first time this thought had passed through my mind today. I'd thought about it this morning over breakfast. Then on the way up the coast. Then many times as we got close enough in the antique mall, and throughout the movie. Yet I hadn't done it. I'd restrained myself. Even when she'd slipped her hand slowly into mine, I'd held back.

"I think I can do that," I whispered. "Of course, you can always call me as well."

She nodded and bit her bottom lip as she stared into my eyes.

Her eyes said everything I needed to know. I could feel the push and pull between us. It hadn't been my imagination; it had gotten progressively stronger all day, and now it was so strong I couldn't fight it any longer. The room grew quiet, the noise from the TV falling away, and I swallowed hard. I leaned in slowly, bringing my lips to hers, grazing them.

My body instantly lit up as her lips met mine. The kiss started out slow, each of us unsure. I didn't move; I didn't want to scare her, but when I felt her left hand slide around my waist and the right rest against my chest, I claimed her mouth.

She let out a small moan and gripped the front of my shirt as I swept my tongue through her mouth. I pulled her tightly against me, kissing her harder when someone knocked on the door.

Our lips parted, and I brushed a loose strand of hair from her eyes as she looked up at me. "Want me to get that?" I asked quietly, silently praying she said no.

Another knock, this one a little more urgent. I looked down at her and she nodded her head.

I unlocked the door and pulled the door open to see a woman I vaguely recognized but couldn't place. She stood there in sweatpants and a sweatshirt. Her hair was an absolute mess, and she was holding a small, sleeping child.

"Oh. I'm..." She glanced at the number on the door. "Um, is Bella..."

I felt Bella's body press up against mine and her hand on my arm as she peeked her head around me. "Brie, is everything okay?" she questioned, alarm filling her voice.

"The alarm went off at The Cooling Rack, Sawyers at work and, well, I have to go. Can Emma stay here with you? I'm sorry to... um... ruin your evening," she said, glancing to me, then back to Bella.

"Of course, she can stay. You're not interrupting anything. Asher was just—"

"I was just on my way home. If you'd like, I can drive you over. I mean, that way you aren't heading there alone," I offered.

Brie looked at Bella and then at me. "That is very nice, but I'll be okay."

"You're sure? Really, it's no trouble."

"Yeah, Brie, you probably shouldn't go alone. Let Asher take you. Here, give me Emma," Bella said, stepping forward and taking the baby from her.

"Thank you."

Bella held on to Emma as I turned and glanced at her. "I'll talk to you tomorrow," I whispered, then leaned in and kissed her cheek.

"I look forward to it," Bella whispered, and then quietly closed her door.

Bella

"HAVE YOU HEARD FROM HIM YET?" Brielle questioned.

Of all the times for her to knock on my door, it had to be when Asher had finally kissed me. Our first kiss had been interrupted by the only person who had tried so hard to get me on a date with someone. "No, not yet. He told me he had to go out of town."

I'd told Brielle nothing about what had happened before she opened the door, and I'd tried to play the kiss on the cheek as just a friendly good-bye. She was skeptical and had kept asking me all these questions.

"Well, hopefully, tonight then. You'll need to let me know." She giggled.

"I will. Listen, I've got to lock up. I'll call you a little later?"

"Sounds good."

When I hung up the phone, I went to the front of the store and locked the door. I'd just made it back into the office when my phone vibrated in my back pocket. I pulled it out and looked to see if Brielle was messaging me to tell me something she'd forgotten and was surprised to see Asher's name on my screen.

He'd told me he was going to be busy the past week and that he had to go out of town for the better part of it. He said he had some business ends to tie up, and he had to meet up with his ex to finish closing out their shared apartment lease.

I'd messaged him twice during that time, but he'd remained quiet. I figured perhaps everything had been too much for him and had decided to just leave him alone.

ASHER: Up for some drinks?

I smiled, looking around at what little I had left to do. It had been a long week, and I hadn't been able to forget that kiss he'd delivered the night Brie had appeared at my door. In fact, I'd woken up many times this week imagining his lips on mine. He was an amazing kisser.

BELLA: Love to.

I watched as those three little dots jumped around for what felt like forever.

ASHER: 205 Water Road

BELLA: Give me twenty minutes

ASHER: I'll be waiting.

I smiled and went about doing what needed to be done, and within five minutes, I was out in my car, heading toward Water Road.

I was just about to knock on the door when it opened and Asher stood before me, a welcoming smile on his face. "Hey."

I smiled and stepped into the front door. As he closed it, he turned and wrapped his arms around me. "Good to see you."

The scent of his cologne invaded my senses as I wrapped my arms around him. When I went to pull away, he leaned in and kissed my lips.

"Come, let's grab a drink and head out back," he said, gently placing his large hand on the small of my back and guiding me to the kitchen.

His backyard looked out over the water and was perfectly lit. "You set all this up?" I questioned.

"No, I'm just renting, remember? Apparently, the people I'm renting this place from normally only rent it out to tourists for weekends. I got very lucky. They had no reservations when I inquired, so I took it for the entire summer. It is beautiful, isn't it?"

"Yes, I'd love to own something like this one day. A small piece of heaven, my own little postage stamp, if you will."

"Same here. So, what is new? How have you been?"

"Not too much. I filled in for Brie today, open to close. I've actually been doing that for most of this week. Emma came down with the flu."

"Oh, well, why didn't you say anything? We could have done this another night," Asher said, sitting forward, a look of concern on his face.

I smiled, biting my bottom lip. "I could have, but I'm really not that tired," I said, drinking the last few drops of the gin and tonic Asher had made for me. "So, what about you? What have you been up to all week?"

Asher stretched, drinking back the last of his beer. "I was in negotiations. Two business contracts, both of which are almost completed."

"So, what is it you do?" I couldn't believe I'd never asked him before now.

"I'm a doctor. After my separation from my girlfriend, I decided that I no longer wanted to stay in the area, so I sold my practice and started looking for a new opportunity. One sort of fell on my lap, so once things have been finalized, I'll be setting down roots."

"That must take up a lot of your time Your practice?"

"A little, but I love what I do."

"That's good," I said, softly smiling, even though I was feeling a little defeated that perhaps our time was coming close to an end. Yet, it wasn't right to let it defeat me. We started out as friends, we'd kissed, we'd also agreed that neither of us was looking for anything. I'd told myself if something happened, it happened, and that this was part of my healing journey. Yet, after spending this time with him, kissing him, I couldn't help but feel that if things were different, I would've given us a chance.

"Then I had the joy of having to deal with my ex."

"How was that?"

He chuckled. "How is it when dealing with yours?"

"Yeah, no need to answer that question." I giggled.

"So, you never told me. How long are you in Eastport for? Is it a permanent move or a temporary one?" he questioned.

"Well, right now, until the end of the summer. My old job might bring me back on board. At least that was what I was told."

"Then what?"

"Well, then I'd move back to Boston. Although I'm still not sure if that is what I want." I shrugged. "I guess I will figure that out when and if the opportunity presents itself." I smiled.

Asher nodded and looked up at the night sky. "It's beginning to cloud over. Looks like it may even rain."

I looked up to the sky to see a dark-grey cloud looming overhead. "Yep, those are definitely storm clouds," I agreed.

"Did you want to head in and catch a movie or something?"

I nodded at the same time I felt a drop of rain hit my arm. "That sounds like a good idea. I just felt a drop of rain."

"Alright, after you," he said, standing.

I bent down and grabbed my glass, then made my way to his back door and stepped inside and placed our glasses down on the counter.

In a matter of moments, we were on the couch, surfing through Netflix's suggestions, debating what to watch while munching on popcorn. We finally agreed on one selection we had passed up from the other night.

"Are you sure you have it in you to watch a thriller and then drive home alone?" He chuckled as the eerie music played during the credits.

"I hope so." I giggled.

Asher leaned back against the couch and placed his arm behind me just as I leaned back. The credits had barely finished when a loud crack of thunder erupted, shaking the windows, causing me to jump.

"Wow, that is some crazy-ass thunder," Asher said,

looking at me before pulling me close. "Are you okay? You must have jumped a mile."

Another rumble hit. I jumped again, and this time the TV went blank. He reached for the remote, pressing some buttons. "Damn, it looks like I've lost internet."

"We aren't having much luck tonight, are we?"

He shook his head and threw the remote down on the couch beside him, leaned back, and rubbed his hand over his face. Just then, another crack of thunder hit, and the room was plunged into darkness.

I shrugged. "I don't know... this is kind of nice," I said, running my hand over his hand.

His eyes met mine. There was nothing left to say between us. He slowly leaned forward, and once again the memory of that kiss came flooding back as his lips meant mine. Everything fell away in that moment.

Lying beside him on the couch, I allowed myself to get lost in his kiss and his touch. I could feel his arousal pressing into my leg, and each time his fingers grazed my bare skin, shock waves flew through my body. It had been so long since I'd been kissed and touched like this, I could barely contain myself. Every part of me was on fire.

"Want to go where we will be more comfortable?" he whispered in my ear before letting his lips dance down my neck.

I tilted my head back, my eyes closed. All I heard myself murmur was yes, as his hands gripped my hips.

He tore his lips from the spot on my neck and stood up. Taking hold of my hand, he gently pulled me through the dark living room and down the hall to his bedroom. He didn't give me time to think, almost as if he knew I'd change my mind.

Once in the room, he closed the door behind us and took hold of me. Placing me up against the door, he kissed me hard. I didn't hear the thunder, but when I opened my eyes, his small bedside lamp was on. He guided me to the bed and sat me down.

I watched as he pulled his shirt off over his head one-handed, exposing his muscular chest and very well-defined six-pack. His eyes were filled with want, and I bit my bottom lip as he took hold of my hands and pulled me to him, the feel of his warm skin comforting me.

My body tingled when his fingers grazed the skin on my sides as he slowly lifted my shirt off me. He dropped it to the floor, and I watched his eyes roam over my body. That was it, he didn't go for more. Instead, he pulled me into his arms, wrapped them around me, and kissed me hard.

I SLOWLY OPENED my eyes and stretched, my body hurting in places it hadn't been yesterday. I looked around the unfamiliar room, the events of last night coming to me. We'd started out slow, and soon we were both breathing hard and writhing against one another. I smiled at the memory and looked over to the other side of the bed, expecting to find Asher still asleep, but saw nothing but a pile of messed blankets. I sat up, listening hard. Nothing but silence surrounded me.

I swallowed hard. Had he left? Why would he leave me here in his house? That was when I heard a clatter of dishes and a muttered curse word.

I lay back in the bed just as the bedroom door opened and his deep voice greeted me. "Morning."

I stretched, sat up, and smiled as he carried a full tray toward me. The first thing I noticed was the small vase of flowers that sat on the tray. "Morning."

"Thought you might like some coffee and some food," he said, placing the tray down at the foot of the bed. He picked up one mug and brought it over to me.

"Thank you." I smiled, taking the mug from him and inhaling the scent of the hot coffee.

I watched as he grabbed his cup and sat down beside me. "So, is everything good?" he questioned. "Was last night okay for you?"

I nodded, taking a sip of the hot coffee.

"It was amazing for me as well."

I could feel the blush rising to my cheeks, Miles had never once asked me if the sex was okay, and he'd never told me if he liked it. "It was more than okay," I said, swallowing hard.

"You're sure?"

"Yeah. Are you sure it was okay for you?"

I watched as Asher nodded. "No, it was. I figured you might be a little wigged out this morning... you know... after the condom broke last night."

Instantly, my eyes fell to the mug in my hands, and I let out a breath. I hadn't told him anything about my divorce, simply that I was, in fact, divorced.

"Bella?" Asher said, bending to catch my eyes. "If it's bothering you, you can tell me."

I sniffled and rubbed my nose, trying hard not to let the past five years of my life come flooding forward. "No, but I can tell you, you don't need to worry about that, like, at all."

Asher looked at me. "You on the pill?" he questioned.

I shook my head.

He frowned. "Why is it that if you aren't on the pill then I don't need to worry?"

I blew out a breath. "I'm infertile." The words rolled off my tongue as if they meant nothing. "So, there's no need to worry about a silly condom breaking," I said, putting on a brave face and meeting his eyes.

He said nothing else. He just picked up the plate that was filled with fruit slices, setting it between us.

"Aren't you going to say anything?"

"There isn't anything to say. I understand. Remember, I'm a doctor. I just didn't want you to be freaking out and think that I didn't care, because I do," he whispered, then leaned forward and kissed me.

As we sat there, he changed the subject, talking about the next exciting adventure he wanted to go on this summer and how he was hoping I'd join him. I smiled and laughed, nodding at what he said, but somewhere deep inside, I couldn't help but wonder how it was he was so understanding about what I'd told him. Sure, he was a doctor, and of course, we were nothing to one another except friends, or now friends with benefits. Perhaps, it had lifted a weight off him as well, the fear of being stuck in some sort of relationship because of some accidental condom mishap.

As much as I worried over that little incident over the coming weeks, things didn't seem to change between us. We began spending more time together. Asher would come and wait at The Cooling Rack until my shift was over, and we'd head to the drive-in. We began spending weekends together instead of just evenings, and while I didn't want to admit it to myself, I knew I was beginning to fall in love with him.

Asher

I'd noticed the first sign of fall this morning while I was on my jog, which meant summer was ending. I'd just finished setting up my office on the thirteenth floor of Eastport General. It had taken way longer to complete the business purchase. So long, in fact, I'd held off on renting this space, in case things didn't go through.

Once all of that had been completed, I reached out to the owners of the small home I'd been staying in. I was more than comfortable there and wanted to see if they would consider selling it. I guess my timing was right because they were more than happy to sit down and work out a deal, and after work today I was to swing by and sign the paperwork.

Now that everything had fallen into place with work, I had one last thing to figure out: Where I wanted to take things with Bella. We'd spent an amazing time together this summer, and now that I knew I'd be living here, it was time to talk to her about us. I wanted something more with her—a lot more. I had mentioned nothing to her yet because I wanted it to be a surprise that I was staying in Eastport. A day hadn't gone by that I hadn't seen her or thought of her since we'd had sex the first time. I was lucky to have her in my life, and I realized she was too good to lose. However, this past week, things seemed to have been off between us. She seemed distracted and distant, and no matter how many times I'd asked her, all she'd say was not to worry. I was worried. I wondered if her perhaps her boss had called and she was worried about telling me she was going back to her job. I couldn't worry about it any longer, so I'd booked us reservations at a steak house for dinner tonight. I picked up my phone and shot her a text.

ASHER: Dinner, tonight, 7pm?

BELLA: Can I call you?

I frowned as I watched those three little dots jump around, then disappear, then jump around again.

ASHER: Yes, of course.

Only when the phone didn't ring right away, I decided to just call her.

She answered the phone, all out of breath. "Hey." She sniffled.

"Hey, everything okay?"

"No, I'm sorry if I've been distracted this week. It's my mom. She's in the hospital. Stage four cancer. I have to go to Columbus and care for her. She needs help, and I'm the only one. I was just on the phone with the airport booking a flight. I did ask that they get me on an earlier one, but for now, I'll be leaving on Friday."

My heart sank for her. My heart sank for me because that meant she would be leaving. "How long will you be gone?" I questioned.

"I've given Brielle my notice. I do not know when I'll be back... or if." She sniffled. "I even gave up my condo. I've been staying with Brie and Sawyer."

The other end of the phone went silent. I swallowed hard. This wasn't how this was supposed to go, and hearing her say those words to me made my heart flip. "How is your mother?"

"Well, the chemo has stopped working. Doctors aren't very optimistic." She sniffled again.

I wanted to be there for her. I wanted her to know I'd be here always. It was on the tip of my tongue to tell her I'd find an oncologist here for her mother to see, but since

I was new here, I really didn't know anyone at the hospital yet.

"I'm sorry. Is there anything I can do?"

"Do you have a magic wand that will help me find a job out in Columbus and—" I heard a sob catch in her throat and the phone went quiet. "I'll see you tonight at 7?"

"If you'd prefer not going, we can always—"

"No, I really could use the time out. I've been crying for hours. It will do me good. It will do me good to be with you. Besides, I asked the airport to get me on an earlier flight if they could."

"Okay, I'll see you at seven."

I shoved my phone into my pocket and finished unloading the last of my books into the bookshelves in my office. Then I turned and looked out the window, taking in the view and thinking about what Bella was going through.

"Oh, Asher," Maureen said, popping her head into my office.

I looked up at my new receptionist. "Yes?"

"Mrs. Becker called. She has an appointment with you on Tuesday. She was wondering if her blood work had come back. Apparently, Dr. Kavanaugh was supposed to call her with the results."

I hadn't even gone through the pending files yet. Maureen had been busy booking appointments for me for the last two days. All the pending files still sat in a box on the floor in the corner of my office. I'd planned to go through them over the weekend.

"Call her back and tell her that the results haven't been sent through to me yet, that I am working on it. Let her know we will discuss everything on Tuesday."

"And Mrs. Lynch?"

I chuckled. I finally felt like I was at home. I'd missed this. "Tell her the same." I smiled, walking over and grabbing the box of files from the floor. "I guess I'll just start going through them now."

"Looks like you have your work cut out for you," Maureen said, looking at the box full of files.

"Thanks, Maureen, and thank you for all the organizing you've been doing."

"Of course, Asher." She smiled.

I looked down at my cell phone to see a text had come in. It hadn't been there prior, and I opened the message. It was from Bella.

> BELLA: I just got off the phone with the airport, they got me on an earlier flight. Do you think you can drive me to the airport tomorrow morning?

I swallowed hard. Tears blurred my eyes. I really wasn't prepared for this to be our last night together.

I STRADDLED HER NAKED BODY, digging my hands into her shoulders. I added more oil to my hands and rubbed her upper back.

"Oh God, that feels good," she whispered.

"That's it, just relax." I continued running my hands over her back, digging into the tight muscles. "You are so beautiful," I said, bending down and kissing her shoulder before I lay beside her.

"I wish things were different," she said, a hint of a tear in the corner of her eye.

I wiped the moisture away. I didn't want her to cry. Instead, I kissed her, my tongue washing through her mouth, hoping to distract her from those thoughts.

"Make love to me," she whispered. "Give me that just one time."

She looked up into my eyes. She didn't need to ask

twice. She didn't need to ask me once. I kissed her as I climbed between her legs. She watched me as I gripped my cock in my hand and found her opening, sliding into her.

I went slowly, wanting her to feel my connection, my passion, my feelings for her. She dug her nails into my back as I pumped into her, slow and hard. A small moan escaping her lips with each pump.

"God, Bella, it feels so damn good."

She gripped my back as I slowed my pace a little. I stilled my hips and took a moment to suck on her perfect nipples. My cock throbbed inside of her as she tightened around me. I began pumping into her again, slowly at just the perfect angle.

"Asher... it feels... so... good. Don't stop doing that," she cried.

I continued at the same pace I was going before, even quickening it a little, then slowing down again. I could feel her fingers gripping into my back as she tightened around me.

"I can't hold back... Asher..."

"Don't hold back..."

Soon she was writhing below me, calling my name as I poured myself into her once again.

We showered together, meeting once again in the shower. She was like a drug that I knew I might not have again. My body, my soul, craved her, and I planned to take every opportunity I had until I could no longer have her again.

She was quiet as we dressed. I'd made us coffee and brought her a mug, and while she dried her hair, I stood in the bathroom door watching her. Every part of me wanted to take away the sadness in her eyes. I wanted to see her smile again.

Time passed faster than I'd wanted, and an hour later, we stood facing one another in the airport. I didn't want to say good-bye, yet I knew delaying it was only going to make it that much harder.

"Thank you for a truly amazing summer." She stepped into me, wrapping her arms around my neck and pressing her body against mine. "I don't want to say good-bye," she whispered, placing her nose in the crook of my neck.

"I don't either," I whispered back, pulling her tighter into me.

I kept my hold on her until I felt hers loosen. She looked up at me with sad eyes, even though she was smiling.

"You have my number if you need anything," I whispered to her.

She nodded. "I do. Thank you. Good luck with everything," she replied. "I hope everything works out for you and that you find the office of your dreams."

I still hadn't told her. I couldn't, not with everything she was dealing with. I feared she would look at it as a tactic to get her to return. I wanted the best for her, and if that meant going to Columbus and creating a life for herself, then so be it. We'd find our way back to one another if it was meant to be. However, when she looked at me this time, it made me feel guilty for not telling her. "And for you," I said.

She leaned in and gave me one last kiss, then turned and handed her boarding pass to the agent at the booth. I watched, and with one last wave, she was gone.

Bella

I SAT in the hospital waiting room fishing for a magazine, any magazine I hadn't read yet. I'd been in Columbus for a month, and I'd spent every single bit of time in this hospital. Mom had been in a lot of pain today, and the doctors had finally given her some pain medication to help. She'd fallen into a deep sleep, but I still felt I needed to be here.

I got up, stretched, and wandered over to another table, searching through the magazines that lay there. None of them were new. I yawned and flopped back down in the chair I'd been sitting in and looked at my phone. It was a little past seven. I'd now been in the hospital for almost ten hours. I let out a breath and checked my messages. I'd had my phone on silent for most of the day, but there was nothing.

"Bella."

I turned to see my mother's doctor standing in the doorway. "Oh, hi, doctor."

"I'm surprised to see you still here."

I shrugged. "It doesn't feel right going home. She was so uncomfortable today."

The doctor made his way over and sat down beside me. "Bella, you need to get your rest. Your mother is resting comfortably, and she is in excellent hands. We will call if there are any changes."

I wiped the stray tear that fell down my cheek. "I guess I just don't want to be alone." I smiled, even though I wanted to cry my guts out. "At least here there is noise and the occasional staff member."

"I see. Is there anyone here that you can call? A friend perhaps."

I shook my head. "All my friends are back in Eastport and Boston. I don't know anyone here. Only my mother."

A throat cleared behind us. I didn't bother to turn around; I figured it was the nurse or another doctor coming to speak with my mother's doctor.

"She doesn't have to be alone, at least for the night, anyway," I heard a familiar voice say.

I turned and looked, not believing my eyes. Asher stood in the waiting room, a concerned look on his face. I didn't hesitate; I jumped up out of the chair and ran over to him, throwing my arms around him.

"My God, what are you doing here?" I cried, hugging him as tight as I could.

"I'll leave you two alone. Take care of her tonight, would you?" the doctor said before leaving the room.

It felt like forever that we'd stood there holding one another. Then Asher guided me over to the chair and sat down.

"What are you doing here?" I questioned, wiping the tears off my cheeks.

"I'm here for a conference."

"Why didn't you tell me?"

"Well, I wasn't sure until yesterday that I could be here, to be honest. So, I decided that if I was able, I'd surprise you. I checked with admissions to see what floor your mom was on and came up. Have you eaten anything?"

I shook my head. I hadn't been taking care of myself at all. Most days I'd lived on a piece of toast or an apple.

"Well, how about you get your things and come stay with me for the night? I have a room at the Hyatt, just across the street."

I wrapped my arms around his neck, still not believing he was sitting in front of me. "I'm so glad you are here. I've missed you."

"I missed you as well. Come on, let's go get you something to eat."

WE'D ORDERED in room service and spent the evening lounging in bed watching television. It was a little past ten when the credits rolled on the show we were watching and he shut the TV off, reached up, and shut the light out. He put his arm under my neck and pulled me closer into him.

"Are you sure you're doing okay?" he whispered.

That had been what I was telling him through text. I didn't want him to worry about me. Only with him here now, it was a little hard to prove it. "Not really. It's hard. I'm lonely." I sniffled.

He was quiet for a moment. "I wish I could be here with you. So does Brie. She told me to tell you that. She also told me in an extremely firm text message to tell you not to call Miles."

I couldn't help but let out a laugh. "Why on earth would she think I'd call Miles?"

"I don't know. She seemed to think that you might, for some sort of comfort, I'm guessing."

"Oh my God, he'd be the last person I'd call for comfort. A wall would provide better comfort."

"I guess perhaps she's just concerned and, like me, wishes she could be here."

I grew quiet and snuggled against him. I wished nothing more than to have them both here as a support system; however, life had been testing me in a lot of ways over the past few years, and every time I faced those challenges alone.

"God, why would she think I'd call him," I repeated, rolling away from Asher. "Does she think I'm stupid or something? I mean, would you call your ex if you needed emotional comfort?"

"Not a chance in hell!" Asher chuckled, pulling me back into him.

"What happened between the two of you, anyways?" I questioned. We'd never really talked in depth about either of our situations.

"So many things."

I could see enough of his face from the moonlight that poured through the window that he didn't want to tell me any more than I wanted to tell him what had happened between Miles and myself. I didn't want him to be angry and to ruin the night, so instead I rolled onto my back. "Never mind, it's none of my business."

"Whoa, just a minute. I want to tell you. I just don't want you to think badly of me."

"Why would I think bad of you?"

"Because most women do after I tell them the story."

"There isn't any judgment here," I said, laying back on my side and facing him.

He nodded, then thought for a few minutes, as if trying to figure out the best way to tell me. Then he took in a deep breath and rested his hand on mine.

"Things between Sydney and I were going well. All things were going well. She'd just gotten a promotion, and my practice had been steadily growing since I'd opened it. We'd gotten engaged about six months earlier, and because we weren't able to get away to celebrate our engagement, I'd booked us a weekend away at a bed-and-breakfast for Valentine's Day. We both needed a break—from work, from wedding plans—and just be together. We found our relationship a bit strained, but nothing that was going to break us.

"Anyways, we got to the bed and breakfast, we spent the day out wandering this small town, had did some shopping and took in dinner and we returned to our room. She started talking about our future and how excited she was to start our life together, and then she brought up having my babies. We'd never discussed this before. In fact, she'd never even mentioned wanting children, and before I knew it, I was already living in a sprawling bungalow with a dog, three kids at my feet, and we weren't even married yet."

"So, it just freaked you out?"

"You could say that. Anyway, I guess she could tell from the look on my face that I wasn't sure about this, and she got upset. I tried to explain myself, but she wouldn't hear it, and she went to bed. The next morning, she was more quiet than usual, but she was speaking to me. When we returned from our weekend, she just seemed to act funny.

"This behaviour went on for weeks, so one night after a stressful day, I confronted her about it. She had somehow gotten it in her mind that I didn't want to have kids with her. That she was the problem. I tried to explain myself and tell her that her conversation had made me feel uncomfortable at that moment, since we were just starting our lives together and I wanted to be selfish to start. I wanted it to just be us. Only she just got angrier at that. Then about two months later, she brought the topic up again."

"What happened this time?"

"Well, I'd been dealing with some pretty heavy things at work. I'd just seen two women lose their first babies, and it absolutely devastated both couples. Plus, my sister had just had a miscarriage and was dealing with the emotional side of it, and her husband had become numb. She had no support. It was hard watching and dealing with this situation on a professional level, not to mention trying to be there for my sister.

"I'd just gotten off the phone with my sister one night when Sydney brought it up to me again. I lost my temper and told her I didn't want children and not to bother bringing it up to me again. She went to bed in tears, and the rest is history."

"Why would I judge you for that? Perhaps it was circumstances that made you feel that way."

Asher ran his hand over his face. "No, the more I've thought about it, the more I realized after seeing the things that I see daily and what I'd just seen with my patients and my sister, that my reaction was very truthful. I think ultimately that was what lead us to breaking up. She really wanted kids, and well, I wanted to focus on my career. Honestly, the more she talked about it, and the more time we spent with friends that had kids, the more I realized I didn't want any, and I didn't think it was fair to not tell her. Only when I sat down and told her, it was like I ended her world. We broke up shortly after that. That's why when you told me you couldn't have children, I really didn't find it that big of a deal. I know you thought I did, but I'm good with it."

"I guess it shocked me a little, especially after how Miles reacted to the entire situation," I whispered.

"Some people, Bella, are incapable of understanding. It's not your fault. It's not something you chose. There are many options out there for those who can't have children."

"I know."

He rolled onto his side and met my lips, pulling me tighter against him. "I'm sorry he treated you the way he did over something so insignificant."

I kissed his lips. His words, his understanding soothed

a place in my soul that I needed at that moment. "I'm so glad you are here," I murmured, kissing him again.

"Me too. You're beautiful, Bella."

His kiss this time felt a little different; it was slower, and as his hand cupped my cheek and his other hand held me tight, I wished he'd never let me go.

"I WISH you didn't have to leave already."

"Same. I wish I could stay here with you for a little while longer anyways. You seem calmer than you did when I arrived," Asher said, looking up at me as he threw the protein bar into his bag.

"I am. It's been nice having someone to have dinner with and to go to bed with, even if it was only for a couple of days."

He smiled. "Yes it was. It's been...lonely." He winked.

Lonely didn't even begin to cover it. The most comforting times I had this weekend was when I had been in his arms. They really were my favorite place to be, and I knew I needed to stop thinking that way, because in a few minutes he'd be on his way to his gate, and I'd be returning to my mother's empty, cold apartment.

"How was your mom today."

I shrugged. "Doctors aren't too optimistic. They are giving her four weeks at most," I said, wiping at my eyes.

"Bella, you know if you need me, you can message or call, right?"

When I didn't look at him and respond, he tucked his finger under my chin and raised my head until I was looking at him.

"You can call," he repeated.

"I know. Thank you."

Asher looked up at the departure board and saw his flight was on time and that they'd be boarding shortly. "I have to get going. Make sure you message me." He leaned in and kissed me.

"I will. Safe flight, okay."

"You be safe getting back to your mom's. I don't like the idea of you taking a cab through this city."

"I will."

He looked into my eyes, not saying anything, then one more kiss and he turned and headed toward the agent at the desk. I stood there watching until he'd waved one final time and disappeared through a set of doors.

For some reason, I'd been waiting for the bubble to pop while he'd been here. Once he was gone, I turned and made my way to the front door to hail a cab. Then it hit me. Somehow, this was all too good to be true. I didn't need to wait for the bubble to burst because it already had. I'd been pretending all this time that he was my boyfriend when, in fact, he was only my friend. Wherever it was that I settled, I'd be alone.

Bella

Three Weeks Later

"I HAVE CHICKEN SOUP," Brielle said, coming into the living room at my mom's apartment. "You should have some. It will make you feel better." She placed the bowl down on the table in front of where I was laying. "Come on, sit up."

"I said I'm not hungry," I muttered, the smell of the soup making me feel nauseous.

"Bella, you've barely eaten anything in the past two, possibly three, days. You've been sick, and now you're hardly drinking anything. I've called Sawyer. He told me it's important that I get something into you before you dehydrate," Brie said, sitting down beside me.

Mom had passed away two weeks ago, exactly one week to the day that Asher had left. The end had been brutal to watch and, for her sake, I was glad it was over. She'd been in pain and had done nothing but cry since nothing would stop it. However, everything I had to do now, combined with the funeral, had been too much. I'd passed out the night of her funeral from stress and exhaustion. Thank goodness Brie had been here. She'd called an ambulance, and the doctor at the hospital would only discharge me if she planned to stay with me. The stress of it all, of everything, had been too much.

Then I'd never looked for another place. I'd been too busy looking after Mom, but now her landlord was being unreasonable. He refused to transfer her lease to me because I did not have a job. So now, on top of everything else, I had no place to live as of the end of the month, which was only in a few short days.

Brie had helped me clean up and pack most of the apartment, and I'd donated most of Mom's things to charity. They'd picked up the last of her things today, aside from the living room furniture and my bed and the few dishes I'd kept to get me through until I left. The rest of my things were back in Eastport. Sawyer and Brielle had rented a small storage unit for my things until I set down roots. Not that it mattered. I was still going to be homeless on Friday.

"God, get that soup away from me. I think I'm going to be sick again," I said, getting up and running to the bathroom, my hand over my mouth.

I slammed the door shut, locking it behind me, making it to the toilet just in time.

"Bella, are you okay?"

I lay on the floor in front of the toilet, clutching my stomach. "I'll be—" I heaved into the toilet once again, this time feeling as if my stomach were about to come out of my mouth. There was nothing left in me to throw up.

I was clammy and grabbed a cloth off the edge of the sink from the last time I'd been in here. I needed to wipe this clamminess off me.

"Bella, open the door," Brie cried as she pounded on the door, jiggling the handle.

The bathroom spun as I was about to stand. "I'm dizzy, Brie," I called out.

"Bella, open this door." I heard her jiggle the handle once again.

I slid across the floor and unlocked the door.

Brie shoved it and took one look at me. She bent down and took the cloth from me and ran it under the water. Ringing it out, she placed it on the back of my neck. "Bella, just breathe."

"I have a headache," I mumbled.

"Yes, no doubt. Now come on, let's get you up and get some soup into you," she said, placing her arm around my waist. "It will make you feel better. I promise."

I was so weak she practically carried me back to the living room, sitting me down on the couch. She sat down beside me and held on to the bowl, bringing a spoon full of the liquid to my mouth. I sipped on the salty chicken broth. At first, my stomach turned and my mouth watered, but that was only for a moment. After the second mouthful, I wanted more.

"Sweetie, you need to look after yourself. I know things have been tough," Brie said, putting the spoon back into the soup and bringing it to my mouth again. "I wish you had called me and taken me up on the offer to come and stay with you before your mom passed."

"I know, but you have enough on your plate with The Cooling Rack, Emma, and the baby on the way."

"Yes, and so do you, and you needed help. Never think you can't call us. If I couldn't have been here, Sawyer would have been. We love you, Bella."

Her words made me feel like I was a child. Then the thought of Friday creeped into my mind, and I imagined I'd be living on the side of a road somewhere. "What am I going to do? I don't have anywhere to go," I cried, tears welling into my eyes. "I have no job. I have no money."

"You know you always have somewhere to go."

"No, Brielle, I'm not imposing again."

"No, of course not. I was going to surprise you, but while I've been here, Sawyer has been working with the landlord. Apparently, the same apartment you had is still available, so he is getting your place back. We both agreed to pay for your rent until you get a few checks under your belt. Plus, I still need an assistant manager, so you still have a job."

Tears flooded my eyes. "Really?"

"Yes," Brie said, wrapping her arm around me and pulling me in for a hug. "However, you need to be strong for the trip back. I need you to share the driving time with me. You are coming back home to Eastport."

FRIDAY MORNING HAD COME. Brie and I had packed everything into my car. Since I'd had to leave Eastport so fast, Brie had kept my car and had driven it up when she came for the funeral. She had planned on taking a flight back, but since I was now going with her, we packed up the car.

"Are you still feeling nauseous?" Brie asked as she shoved the last box into the trunk of her car.

"Yeah. I feel stronger, though," I said, taking a drink of the electrolyte drink Sawyer had recommended.

"Good. Sawyer wanted to know if those were helping," she asked, nodding to the green fluid in the bottle I held in my hand.

I nodded. "I just wish they tasted better."

"Yeah, well, he drinks the green one all the time after his workouts. He said you would probably like the blue one better, but that was the only one I could get." She shrugged. "I figured it would be better than nothing. You ready to go?"

"Yes," I said, deciding against going up to the apartment one more time to do nothing but look at the empty rooms.

"You drive first," Brie said, handing me the keys and climbing into the passenger's seat.

Our plan was to drive halfway today, stop for the night at a hotel along the way, then finish the drive tomorrow. We'd stopped and gotten something for breakfast, and half an hour later, as we were driving on the interstate, I felt that familiar gush of saliva in my mouth. I tried to fight it, but the feeling got worse over time, so I pulled over to the side of the road.

"What's wrong?" Brie asked, pulling her head out of her phone.

"I'm gonna be sick again," I said, cutting the engine, ripping my seatbelt off, and shoving the door open.

I just made it to the front of the car and was sick. I leaned against the side of the car, just taking in the air, hoping and praying that some air would calm my stomach down. I could see Brie in the front seat on her phone, no doubt texting Sawyer. I rolled my eyes, wondering what other doctorly advice he had for me now. When I finally felt better, I climbed back into the driver's seat and put my seatbelt on. I was about to start the engine when Brie put her hand on mine.

"How long has this been going on?"

"What?"

"This being sick? How long?"

I shrugged. "I don't know, a couple of weeks maybe."

Brie looked out the window and nodded. "I was speaking with Sawyer just now. He, um, recommends that you take a pregnancy test."

"Is that supposed to be some sort of joke?" I said through blurry, tear-filled eyes. "Why would you even suggest that to me? You know the same as I do that Dr. Kavanaugh told me years ago I was infertile, that there was no way I would ever get pregnant."

Brie closed her eyes and rested her head against the seat. "Doctors can be wrong... Besides, I know that you and Asher...."

"That Asher and I what? That we slept together?"

Brie slowly nodded. "Yes, you didn't need to tell me that. I knew a long time ago, from the way you looked at him. Regardless, you don't have flu symptoms at all. Sawyer also doesn't think this is stress. I hate to admit it, but I agree with him."

"Brielle, I've had enough of this conversation. It's time to get back on the road."

"Bella…"

"No, please, don't," I said, fighting back tears. "I'm shocked you would even suggest that to me. You know how badly—" I stopped. There was no point in even continuing this conversation. She knew how badly I'd wanted a baby. She also knew how hard it had been for me to accept the fact that I would never have one.

I put the car into drive, checked my mirrors, and pulled out onto the road. The silence between us became so loud I turned the radio on. Soon, Brie kept her face down, typing away into her phone, no doubt telling Sawyer everything. He was probably on the phone to that psychiatrist they'd tried to set me up with when I'd first moved to Eastport, booking me in for an appointment instead of a date. I swallowed my hurt and my anger and kept my eyes on the road.

We'd switched up about halfway into the afternoon and finally stopped around eight at a small roadside motel. I would have been just as happy to continue driving through the night, but Brielle insisted I needed to sleep.

Two hours later, I was lying in bed watching TV when Brie came through the door with a bag of snacks. She smiled as she threw the bag down on the bottom of her bed and kicked her shoes off. Sitting down, she pulled out a bag of plain chips, tossing them onto the bed beside me, along with a bottle of soda.

"Thanks," I muttered.

"You're welcome."

I watched as she pulled out a bag of barbeque chips for herself, as well as a bottle of soda, then she carefully folded the bag around something else and set it behind her.

I frowned. "What else do you have in the bag?"

"Oh, just a box of condoms. We're out at home," she said, giving me an odd smile.

I looked at her and rolled my eyes. "I've seen condoms before, you know. You don't need to hide them as if they are a national treasure. Plus, I don't think they are really necessary at this point," I said, nodding to her small baby bump.

Her face went red, and she gave me an awkward smile. "So, when was the last time you spoke to Asher?"

I tore the bag of chips open and shrugged as I shoved one into my mouth. "I don't know. I guess it would have been right after my mom passed."

"You mean he hasn't messaged you at all?"

"No, he has." I hadn't told her about the weekend he'd been in Columbus. She didn't need to know about it, because I was certain I'd never hear the end about the pregnancy test.

"And..."

"And what?

"Are you two an item?"

I shook my head. "We agreed that neither of us were looking for anything. It was more of a healing journey. Honestly, it's exactly what I expected. That we'd keep in touch, as friends."

"So, he's the one who messaged you. Does that mean you haven't even tried to contact him?"

I shook my head. "I have, but honestly, there is no point. He was starting his new chapter, and I was starting mine. I need to get some rest." I folded the bag of chips closed, reached up and shut the light off and rolled over onto my side, facing away from Brie. After I set my alarm, I opened my text messages to see Asher's name. I clicked the messages open, reading the ones he'd sent.

> ASHER: I hope everything is going okay. It's been a few days since I heard from you. When you get some time, message me. Thinking of you.

> ASHER: Hey Bella, I'm sure you are busy with the funeral and everything. Please, when you get a free moment, message me, I want to talk to you about something.

ASHER: I'm getting the weird feeling
that you don't want to talk to me. I
hope that isn't the case. Please let me
know how you are doing. I want you
to know that I am here for you.

ASHER: Letting you know I'm thinking
of you.

I blinked hard, clearing the tears from my eyes. He'd sent the last message this afternoon. The rest, I just hadn't had the energy to respond to. Plus, I was afraid of what it was he wanted to talk to me about. I had turned my entire world, as small as it was, upside down, and as much as it hurt me not to respond, I figured it was for the best. I couldn't take any more disappointment. After all, even though I was on my way back to Eastport, Asher had left. I now needed to focus on my path of starting our lives over.

THE SCENT of bacon and eggs woke me. I stretched, rolling over. Brie sat at the small table in our room, digging into a plastic container of food.

"Ah, you're awake. I went to the small diner across the street and brought back breakfast."

"What time is it?" I questioned, still noting it was dark outside.

"A little after five."

I'd set my alarm for six; I wasn't ready to get up yet. I just wanted to close my eyes and stay curled up under these blankets, but I knew I couldn't, so I kicked the covers off and made my way over to the table. I looked down at the food through the clear lid of the plastic container and opened it. The smell of steamed eggs wasn't very appealing.

The smell got worse as I dug the fork into the eggs. I sat back, trying to avoid the smell, and opened the lid on the paper cup that contained a coffee. I dumped two packets of sugar and two creamers into it and stirred it, then took a sip.

"You not hungry?" Brie questioned.

I shrugged and picked up a piece of bacon, taking a bite. Knowing she was watching me like a hawk, I took my fork and dug into the messy pile of scrambled eggs again. The second the eggs hit my tongue, my stomach turned. I tried to fight it by shoving another mouthful of eggs into my mouth, but that only made it worse. I spit the eggs back into the container and took off in a mad dash toward the bathroom.

A few minutes later, I stepped back into the room and looked at Brie, who sat there with a knowing look on her face. She said nothing. She just reached for the bag she had wrapped up last night and pulled out a pregnancy test.

She stood up, walked over to me, and shoved it into my hand.

"I thought you said this was a box of condoms?"

"Well... I lied. Now, humour me, would you?" she said, nodding to the bathroom.

Minutes later, I sat there in disbelief as I looked down at both of the little white sticks, both showing the same result. Double pink lines stared back at me. I'd taken both. I figured the first one was faulty, but when the second one produced the same result, all I could do was stare. Brielle had been right.

"Well?" Brie called from the other side of the door. "You've been in there a long time. I can't take the suspense."

I tore my gaze away from those two white sticks and looked at myself in the mirror. *What mess had I gotten myself into?* I stormed out of the bathroom, shoving past Brie and heading for the door. I stepped outside and pulled the door closed behind me, taking in the fresh morning air. I walked over to the railing and leaned against it, looking out over the parking lot. My mind was racing with all kinds of thoughts.

"It's going to be okay, you know," Brie said, placing her hand on my shoulder.

I let out a little laugh. "Why is that? Because it worked out for you?"

Brie said nothing. I didn't want to hear it. I'd spent

years trying to get pregnant with Miles, looking at the disappointment on his face every single time one of these tests came back negative. It had torn us apart.

My family doctor in Boston had sent me to Dr. Kavanaugh in Eastport, and he'd been the one who determined I was infertile. Miles at first refused to believe it, and every time we'd have sex, it was only to try once again to have the same outcome. Anger coursed through my body as I thought about his diagnosis. The depression I'd went through, all the hateful words Miles had said to me in the last two years of our marriage. The lack of love he'd given me had created a pit in me so deep, I feared it would be impossible for me to get out of. And for what? Now that I was almost out of it, I find out that none of it was true. Now I was pregnant, and Asher was the opposite of Miles; he didn't want to have children.

"Are you going to call Asher?"

I shook my head. "Nope. I'm going to call Dr. Kavanaugh."

Brie frowned. "Bella..."

"We should get going. It's getting late, and we can probably beat some of the traffic."

"Bella? Stop," Brie said, grabbing hold of my arm.

"What?"

"You should call and speak with Asher. Let him know."

"Brielle, I barely know! I don't know anything at this point. I barely know what I'm doing tomorrow."

"Bella..."

I looked at her and let out a sigh. "Why should I message him? So he can be cold and heartless? No thanks. I had one man treat me that way. I refuse to allow another."

"Whoa, when was he mean to you?"

He hadn't been mean yet, but I was certain that if he found out about this baby, that would change. I hadn't told Brielle about him not wanting kids, because that would mean I'd have to explain that he'd been in Columbus. Besides, once he'd explained it to me, it made me feel that someone could accept my situation.

"He hasn't been... yet."

Brie frowned. "What's going on, Bella? Asher seemed to really adore you. I can't imagine that he'd be mean to you in any way."

I looked at Brielle, considering what she was saying, but I also knew she was wrong. I let out a breath. "Yeah, well, that might be true, but I know if I tell him this, the Asher who adored me won't be the same one to respond."

Bella

I'D BEEN BACK in Eastport for four days. Sawyer and Brie had made sure what little I'd had in the small storage facility in Eastport was delivered to my place on Monday.

I'd unpacked the last of the boxes last night after I'd gotten home from The Cooling Rack. It was a beautiful fall day, and I sat out on my balcony enjoying a warm cup of tea with some arrowroot cookies, while I waited for the dryer to finish.

I reached for my phone and looked up Dr. Kavanaugh's number, then hit the call button. After three rings, I heard a woman answer. "Hello."

"Hi, I need to book an appointment with Dr. Kavanaugh. It's Bella Langdon."

"One moment, please."

I sat listening to the god-awful jazz music that played

on the other end of the line, and I took a bite of cookie, followed by a sip of tea.

"Ah, yes, Miss Langdon. Did you receive a letter in the mail?" the friendly voice asked.

I glanced at the stack of mail on the small table inside the living room. I hadn't looked at the stack of mail Brie and Sawyer had collected. "Ah, not that I know of."

"We mailed it to your address in Boston."

"No, I'm sorry. I've moved recently," I said, glancing at the pile of mail that Sawyer had brought back from Boston with him earlier in the summer. I'd glanced through it. Nothing seemed to be all that important, and I wondered if perhaps I'd missed it.

"Oh, okay then. Well, Dr. Kavanaugh has retired."

"Oh. I see. Well, I need a doctor. Is it possible that whoever took over could see me?"

"Please give me a moment."

Suddenly, that horrible music returned. As I sat there, I could feel the tension in my shoulders. I just so badly needed clarification, and I hoped they had transferred my entire file. I needed to know what had happened, or where the mistake was.

"Bella, I can see we have transferred your file to Dr. Alonzo Love. He actually has an opening Thursday morning at ten thirty. Can you tell me what this is regarding, so I have some information to mark down. Also, it will help me figure out if you need any blood work prior to the appointment."

"I'm pregnant," I blurted. No matter how many times I said it, the situation still didn't sound right.

She cleared her throat and said, "I see... but it states here that—"

"I know what it states, which is part of the problem," I bit out. I didn't need some receptionist to tell me what was written in my file.

"Miss Langdon, are you able to head down to the lab at Eastport General sometime today or tomorrow to have some blood work done? That way, we can have your results for the appointment."

"Yep."

"And do you know where our office is?"

I let out a sigh. "I'm guessing it's still in the same place."

"Actually, it's in the hospital, thirteenth floor. Just go to the main elevators and take it up to thirteen. You'll turn right and then make a left at the first corridor. The office is on the right-hand side."

"Okay."

"We will see you Thursday, Bella."

I reached over and picked up a magazine that lay on the table. It was the only magazine in the entire office that wasn't about parenting or pregnancy. I let out a sigh as I flipped it open and began looking at ideas on how to organize a kitchen. I was doing everything I could to distract myself from thinking about my blood work results.

I'd wanted to call all day yesterday to find out, yet I knew they probably wouldn't share those results with me over the phone. A door opened and out came a very pregnant woman, a smile on her face as she said good-bye to the nurse who'd walked her out. I placed the magazine down on the table and rubbed my hands together.

"Bella Langdon?" the nurse called.

I closed my eyes, took in a deep breath, and stood up.

"Hello, Bella, follow me, please."

I followed her down a hall where she stopped at the first door she came to and opened it up. "Take a seat. The doctor will be with you shortly," she said, placing my file in the hanging folder on the door.

As I sat there looking around, my eyes kept landing on my file that sat in the holder on the door. I could always just take a quick peek, I thought to myself. When I had just about built up the nerve, I heard a door open and the doctor appeared.

"Bella. I'm Dr. Alonzo Love." He opened the file and looked over a couple of things before he shut the door. He smiled at me and then sat down behind his computer. "So, what is bringing you in today?"

"Well..." I looked around the room and rubbed my hands together, trying to gather my thoughts. "Sorry, I'm a little nervous."

"No need to be. This is a safe space. Take your time." He smiled at me and sat back against the chair.

"A few years ago, I was having a hard time trying to conceive, and Dr. Kavanaugh diagnosed me as being infertile. It seems, though, that perhaps the diagnosis was incorrect, and well, after being intimate with someone recently, it seems I am pregnant."

"I see. So, what did Dr. Kavanaugh say the cause of the infertility was? Did he do any tests?" he said, glancing down to my file.

"From what I remember, he didn't say what the cause was. He did some blood work, other than that, nothing. My ex-husband and I at the time were trying to have children, and I just couldn't conceive."

"I see. Do you think the problem could have been him?"

"I don't know. He said it was all me." I shrugged.

"Who did? Dr. Kavanaugh?"

"No, my ex. He was irritated, perhaps disappointed, and he booked me in with my family doctor, who sent me to Dr. Kavanaugh. After the blood work that Dr.

Kavanaugh ordered came back, he told me I couldn't have children."

"So, he did no other tests, no ovulation testing, no hormone testing, imaging tests?"

"No."

Dr. Love flipped through my file, studying my history, then he stopped to look at what I hoped was my most recent blood work report. "Well, Bella, I can tell you that your recent blood work came back, and you are pregnant."

"Hmm." I nodded my head. "I'm sorry, but I'm having a hard time understanding how that is possible."

The doctor sat back and clicked his pen. "Bella, would you say at the time of the diagnosis that you were highly stressed, perhaps a little anxious? That the situation you and your husband were facing was, perhaps, a little more than you could handle at the time?"

A lot anxious and extremely stressed was more like it. Miles wasn't patient or understanding. "Yes, it would be fair to say that."

"Were you at the time being treated for depression when this was going on?"

I nodded and picked at my fingernail as I sat there. "I wasn't on depression medication, but my family doctor said he had noticed changes in me, and he was watching me for signs of depression."

"I see," Doctor Love said, clicking his pen. "Did you know that high periods of stress, anxiety, and depression can severely alter your ability to get pregnant? That it can take years for you to regulate your body again after the stress is gone?"

I shook my head. "I didn't."

"I take it Dr. Kavanaugh didn't mention any of these things to you?"

I shook my head. "He never even hinted at any of those questions."

"I see." Dr. Love made some notes. "How long has your ex been your ex?"

"We are closing in on a year now."

"And how have your stress levels been?"

"Good, aside from recently. My mom just passed away. But I spent most of the summer working with a friend of mine at her bakery and just focusing on myself. I met someone, but I was upfront and honest about what it was I wanted, which was only friendship. It just so happened that things went an unexpected way between us."

"There is nothing wrong with that. Also, self-care is an amazing way to heal. You need to more of that, especially right now, after all the stress of your mom. Which I'd like to say that I am sorry for your loss."

"Thank you."

"I want you to do more of the self-care. I also want to know how your relationship is now with the man you met."

I looked at the doctor, then down to my feet. "At the

moment, I am not sure. He was just out of a terrible relationship as well. We both were on a healing path. At the end of the summer, my mom got sick, and I left Eastport. He'd already told me he was moving out of Eastport. We saw one another three weeks ago or so, and we have spoken through text."

"I see. Does he know about the baby?"

When I didn't answer him right away, he put his pen down and looked at me. "Bella? Does he know about the baby?"

I shook my head. "No. I haven't told him yet. Not sure I am going to."

"I see. Why is that? Do you not think he has a right to know?"

"He, um, he told me he doesn't want children."

Doctor Love nodded, then stood up from behind his desk and came around, leaning on the front of it. "Well, there's lots of time for you to tell him if you change your mind. I think the best thing is for you to take some time and think about it. Don't just decide not to tell him because he doesn't want children. His opinion may change."

"No, it won't."

"Bella there isn't a rush to decide. You have time. Now, I'd like to take your weight and blood-pressure. Then I will have you get changed into this robe for your physical exam."

Doctor Love assured me that everything was fine and booked me in for my next appointment. I left the office feeling better than I had when I arrived and headed to my car. As I climbed in, I placed my purse on the passenger's seat and dropped the appointment card in the cupholder. I did up my seatbelt and then looked down at the appointment card. The date for my next appointment was staring back at me. As I sat there, I realized I didn't know how I felt. I was angry; I was upset; I was excited. These feelings flooded my body. I knew I had the support of Brielle and Sawyer. However, their support didn't mean anywhere near what Asher's would have meant.

There was no point in dwelling on it. He'd only know if I told him, and right now I'd decided against that. I had a lot of things to get organized before I started back to work. I put the key into the ignition, turned on my favourite radio station, and pulled out of the lot, heading toward my condo.

Asher

October

I DROPPED my keys into the dish I kept at the front door and kicked off my sneakers. I'd gotten up early this morning to go for a run. It was my first day off in two months, and as much as I missed my practice when I wasn't working, I hadn't realized how much I'd needed some time off. The last couple of months had been stressful.

It appeared Dr. Kavanaugh had been behind on many appointments, and it had been hell trying to catch up. Every single day, Marie had booked me solid with appointments. I was hoping things would be slow to start;

however, I'd gone at warp speed every day with no signs of things slowing down. I'd been so overbooked that I ended up needing to find an OB/GYN to hire to help with the overflow, plus to help me with the intake of new patients. With that simple change, I'd finally been able to take a day off.

Stripping off my sweat filled T-shirt, I made my way to the bathroom and turned on the shower. I quickly checked my phone, hoping that perhaps Bella had left me a message, but once again, there was nothing. Despite all that had gone on in the last couple of months, work hadn't been the only thing to stress me out. It bothered me that I'd thought of Bella every single day since she'd left, with those thoughts getting stronger since I'd been in Columbus and spent the weekend with her.

She'd never know it, though. I'd messaged her a grand total of four times since I'd left. Four times, it was horrible for me to claim I cared for her. Anyone who looked at the situation would say I only wanted another romp in the sack. I didn't even know if the messages had gone through. For all I knew, she could have changed her number, especially if she'd stayed in Columbus. I'd been so busy with work, I hadn't even had time to stop over at The Cooling Rack. Even though I knew she wouldn't be there, I could have at least inquired with Brielle. Surely, she would have heard something.

I figured today was as good of a day as any to make

that change. I showered, quickly ate breakfast, and then made my way to The Cooling Rack. I had to go into town anyway, as I needed to do some errands.

I pulled into the parking lot. The place was a mess when I walked inside. Dirty dishes were on every table, and the two kids behind the counter didn't seem to care that people were waiting for a seat. Surely, Brielle wasn't here either, if this was the state of the place.

"Can I help you?" the kid behind the counter asked as the other grabbed a bus pan and headed out onto the floor, beginning to clear off the tables and wipe them down.

"Yeah, I'll take a large coffee, and I was wondering if Brielle was here?"

"She isn't here at the moment, but she should be back in shortly," the kid said, placing a paper cup on the counter.

"I think I'll take one of those blueberry scones as well. Also, please put my coffee into a mug. I'm going to just take a seat and wait for Brielle to come in."

The kid looked at me, rolled his eyes, and dumped my coffee into a mug. Then he grabbed a scone from the display case and dropped it onto a plate and put it on the counter.

I'd just sat down and bit into the scone when out of the corner of my eye I was sure I spotted Bella. I looked and, sure enough, walking beside Brielle was Bella. Excitement built in me as I watched them approach the front of the building. I was about to get up and go greet them, but they walked right by the front door.

As they walked by the window, I took in her face. She looked upset, and she was talking frantically, her hands flying around as Brielle listened intently. I wanted to know what it was she was saying. They walked by and continued on their way to the side of the building. They must have been going in the back way, I thought to myself.

I took a sip of my coffee. I could wait, I thought. I had nowhere to be. Not today, anyway. I'd just finished my scone when Brielle stepped through the door. She spoke to the gentlemen who had served me. He said something to her, and her eyes met mine. I waved, only she didn't wave back. Instead, she said something else to the kid and then went back into the kitchen.

A few minutes later, she reappeared and made her way over to my table. "Hey, Asher. How are you? Benny said you wanted to see me."

"Hey, Brielle. Bella, she's back?" I questioned. I wasn't going to beat around the bush. I wanted to see her.

"She is. She's just in the back. I'm not sure if—"

Suddenly, she stopped speaking, and I followed her eyes over to the kitchen door to see Bella standing there, looking at both of us.

I couldn't tell from the look on her face if she was happy to see me or if she was going to run. Brielle said nothing; she just studied her for a moment. My stomach churned with excitement, and when I was sure she was going to back away and run, she surprised me by taking a step forward and making her way to the table.

"Hey, Asher." Her voice was soft, and I hadn't realized how much I'd missed hearing her say my name.

"Bella, you don't need—"

She looked at Brielle and smiled. "It's fine. I'm just going to talk to Asher for a few minutes, then we can have our meeting."

"You sure?" Brielle said, like a protective older sister.

"Yep." She smiled as she met my eyes. "It's fine."

"Okay, I'll have Benny bring over a hot tea and a refill for you, Asher," she said as she got up from where she'd been sitting and made her way behind the counter.

Once the tea and coffee had been delivered at the table, Bella smiled at me. "What are you doing in Eastport?"

I'd hated myself for not telling her before she'd left. After she'd gone, I hated myself, and I couldn't even explain how I felt for not telling her after I'd left her in Columbus. "I hadn't wanted to say anything until I knew for sure everything was a done deal. The night I'd planned to tell you was the night you told me about your mom. It wasn't really a time for celebrating. You were leaving. I was going to tell you in Columbus, and once I saw how upset you were I, once again, waited. That's what I wanted to talk to you about when I'd messaged you. I wanted to tell you I stayed in Eastport, and I opened up a practice here. I hoped that may make you come back."

"Oh. Congratulations. I'm happy for you," she answered. I could see she was uncomfortable, and she sat there running her finger around the rim of the mug that sat in front of her. I was quiet. She had something on her mind. I could see it.

"I wanted to respond to you. To your messages," she whispered.

"Why didn't you?" I questioned.

"It... it was just too hard. You were too far away. It was so hard dealing with my mom, and I knew if I had messaged you, I'd want you to be with me."

Now I felt even worse for not picking up the phone. There had been so many times over the last couple of weeks I'd wanted to call. Each time I'd pick up the phone and dialled, I'd hung up before it had gone through.

"Instead, at night, I'd lay in bed, reading over your messages, then fall into a fit of tears. I figured you'd left Eastport, anyway. Once Mom passed and everything was over, I quickly realized I'd moved there and hadn't even looked for a job. My mom was behind on her rent, and while the landlord was kind enough to allow me to stay there once she passed, he wasn't as willing to work with me. He'd given me time to find a new place to live, but once the first of the month rolled around, he'd asked that I be gone. I had Brielle come and stay with me for a while, to help me pack things up, and she was the one who convinced me to return to Eastport."

"Bella, I'm so sorry. Fuck, I knew I should have called you."

"It's okay," she said, placing her hand on mine. "No doubt you were busy with things here. The last thing you needed to be dealing with was my issues." She shrugged.

"I'm sorry about your mom," I said, taking her hand in mine.

She looked at me and nodded. "Thank you."

"Are you back for good?" I questioned. "Or are you planning just to stay here until something better comes along?"

She nodded. "I'm back for good. Brielle offered me my job back, and Sawyer was able to get my condo back. I took it. What about you? Where are you living?"

"Well, at first, I was going to find a place, but the people who I was renting from ended up selling me the place instead."

"I'm happy for you that things have fallen into place," she said, growing quiet.

She was talking, and I didn't want her to stop. I also didn't want to stop talking. I wanted her to know I was still here, and I wanted her to know I wanted to carry on things from where we left off. She needed to know that she could still trust in me. I cleared my throat. "I'd still like us to be friends."

She nodded, a look of concern on her face.

"Well, perhaps more than friends. I'd like us to try…" I swallowed hard. "I'd really like us to continue from where we left off."

Her eyes met mine. She said nothing; she just sat there looking at me. I grew scared that she was about to turn me down.

Then Brielle popped her head over the back of Bella's seat and smiled. "Perfect. She'd love to. She'd also like to know if you would like to join Sawyer and I for dinner this weekend?"

I glanced at Bella, who closed her eyes and clenched her jaw. I cleared my throat. "Um, I…"

Bella looked at me, then she shook her head. "Brielle, please." Then she turned to me.

"You don't have to," she said, shaking her head.

"Dinner sounds good. What time?" I asked, ignoring what Bella had said.

"Say eight next Friday?"

"Eight on Friday. I'd be happy to join you," I said.

For whatever reason, Bella didn't look happy. Whatever was bothering her, I knew she was doing her best to hide it.

"Eight on Friday," she said, more to herself than to

anyone else. "I really should get to work." She slid out of the booth and stood up.

"I'll message you later?" I questioned.

"Sure... whatever you'd like," she replied, then took both mugs and my plate and made her way over to the counter where she placed them down and grabbed a cloth.

I slid out of the booth and made my way to the door, turning to look at her one more time before I left. She was wiping down tables, a sad look still on her face. I hoped it was only because of her mom and that she was happy to be back. I guessed I'd find out soon enough.

Bella

I LAY in bed Thursday night reading my latest library pick as the TV droned on in the background. Tomorrow night was weighing on my mind as I barely focused on the words. I dropped the book down on the bed beside me and stared up at the ceiling. I'd read the same paragraph three times and still hadn't been able to follow the story. Why had I agreed to dinner this weekend? I should have said no immediately. I didn't want Brielle to put pressure on us. What had I been thinking?

I reached for the glass of water I had beside the bed and took a sip. It was almost one in the morning. Doctor Love had told me he wanted me to get extra rest, which meant going to bed early. I'd been exhausted lately, more than normal, and when I'd shared my concerns with him, he'd popped me on a prenatal vitamin and told me to be in bed by eleven, and earlier on the nights where I had to work earlier the next morning. So far, it wasn't working.

I reached up and turned the light off, hoping that by some miracle laying in the darkness may help me relax enough to fall asleep. Asher had texted me earlier, but I hadn't replied. That too was weighing on my mind.

I reached for my phone. Perhaps if I messaged him now, that would clear enough of my mind to allow for some sleep. He'd be asleep now anyway, I thought to myself, so there wouldn't be a chance he'd message me back until morning.

I skimmed his message again.

> ASHER: I was wondering if you wanted to get out for a coffee?

I tapped the edge of my phone and then typed.

> BELLA: Sorry I just saw this now. I went to the library, and then to the craft store, my phone was in my purse with the ringer off. Raincheck? Say tomorrow night?

After hitting send, I put the phone down on the table and flipped through the TV channels. I'd just found a movie to watch when my phone vibrated against the table, causing me to jump.

As I picked it up, I frowned as I saw a message from Asher. What the hell was he doing up? I opened the phone.

> ASHER: No worries. What are you still doing up this late?

> BELLA: I should ask you the same? Those three little dots bounced around furiously, matching my heartbeat.

> ASHER: Just finished up at the hospital. It was a good thing I was here because I needed help distracting my thoughts from thinking of a certain someone.

I smiled as those three dots bounced around again.

> ASHER: Now why are you still awake?

> BELLA: Can't sleep.

> ASHER: I see…does the doctor need to prescribe something? ;)

I felt my cheeks get warm at his text. I knew I was blushing, and my centre throbbed as I thought about what it was he would prescribe.

BELLA: Perhaps ;)

I sat staring at my phone. Why had I just typed that? It was almost as if I were a glutton for punishment. As I lay there waiting for his reply, I could have kicked myself, and the longer it took for him to respond, the more I'd wished I could actually do just that. After a full minute, those three little dots began bouncing again.

ASHER: Since we both can't sleep do you feel like company?

I bit my bottom lip. We hadn't been alone since those nights in Columbus. The memory of them had sat in the front of my mind ever since. How he'd comforted me, how he held me before, during, and after sex. I'd grown to love being held by him, and for the past week, ever since seeing him at the diner, I'd been dying to feel that again. I'd have died to have had him hold me when my mother passed, but that had been impossible. Now, with a pregnancy looming over my head, I felt I needed him more than ever, and yet I was afraid to tell him for fear he said good-bye.

BELLA: Sure come over

That was all I texted, then immediately I wanted to kick myself again.

ASHER: On my way

I kicked the blankets off me and made my way out into the hallway. The crib Brielle and Sawyer had gotten me earlier this week was leaning against the wall, still in the box. I walked over and tried to move it, but it was too heavy to even drag into the small spare bedroom that would end up being the nursery. Panic filled me. Sawyer was supposed to have come back tonight and move it into the room for me, but he'd had an emergency and wasn't able to, and now I knew Asher would ask questions.

I gave it another try, moving it only an inch. "Shit," I muttered to myself. I thought about getting my phone and just telling Asher I was tired when I heard a quiet knock on the door.

I took a couple of steps and spotted the small bag of baby clothes I'd also purchased laying on the floor. I picked them up and threw them into the spare room before making my way to the door.

"Hey," he said, smiling.

I stepped to the side and let him in, taking his coat and hanging it on the small hooks just inside the door. I shut and locked the door and turned to see him toe his shoes off. He was barely in the door and the scent of his cologne was driving me mad.

We stood in the entryway, looking at one another. Then he stepped toward me, placing his arms around my waist, and pulled me against him for a hug. He was so warm, I could feel his heat through my thin silk pajamas. I buried my face into the crook of his neck as he hugged me tight. God, I'd missed how his body felt against mine. I hadn't really realized it until now. As I stood there, in his arms, our bodies pressed against one another, I knew in a matter of moments I would want more. I'd want to feel his lips on mine and his hands exploring my body until I could no longer stand it. I was about to step away when our eyes locked.

There was no time to stop and rationally think about what I was doing, because my lips were already against his. The kiss broke, both of us breathing hard. We finally pulled away from one another. Then he blew out a deep breath.

"I need to calm down. I didn't just come here for this. I don't want you to think that," he said in a quiet voice as he ran his fingers through his thick, dark hair.

He looked around my dark apartment. "I thought you said you were up when you messaged me?"

"I was, but I was in bed watching TV." I giggled. "Come." I placed my hand in his, hit the light in the hallway, and pulled him down the hall and into my bedroom, shutting the door behind us.

I crawled into bed and watched while he removed his shirt and unbuttoned his jeans. Then he crawled into bed, under the covers, and pulled me into him.

"You know, I thought a lot about you while you were gone. I thought more about us after I left Columbus too."

"You did?"

"I did. I meant what I said earlier this week as well. That I wanted us to continue from where we left things off."

"What does that mean for you?" I questioned.

"I really like you, Bella. We said we were only going to do the friendship thing, but I want more. I want you, and I want to see if we can give a relationship a try."

I was quiet. My head spun. I wanted that so bad. "I don't know," I whispered.

"What don't you know?"

"I don't know if that—if we, are a good idea," I said, swallowing hard.

Asher met my eyes. "Don't say that."

"I can't help it. I'm afraid."

Asher pulled me into him. "Tell me, what would make you less afraid."

Thousands of thoughts flew around my head, while only one of them came forward. The fact that in a few short weeks he'd notice a baby bump.

"You can tell me, you know. Is it something from your past relationship?"

Yep, he'd figured it out. The two men were exact opposites.

"I'm not Miles. I'm not the type to run from problems and place blame where it shouldn't be placed."

"How did you know that he did that?"

"I grew up with him, remember. We may not talk now, but he never changed. He was like that as a kid, he was that way in high school, so I'm sure he's that way now."

"Yes, he is," I whispered.

"You know, I've made mistakes in my past, done things that I wasn't proud of, but with each mistake, I learned to grow. You don't need to worry about me doing those things."

I let out a breath. "I know."

"How about we give it a trial run. Why don't we, after dinner tomorrow night, spend the weekend together. I have the weekend off and so do you. We can stay at my place, go shop, make dinner, watch movies. Just be together?"

"I'd love that," I whispered as he kissed my neck again.

"If that weekend goes well, I know that there's a musical festival coming up. Some of our favorite bands are playing, and I was thinking of getting us tickets. We could get a hotel, spend the weekend away."

"That sounds like fun. I'd love that," I replied, wondering how long it would be before I'd start showing.

I let out a yawn, and Asher reached around behind him and shut the TV off, then pulled the covers up around us and pulled me into him. I closed my eyes and allowed the heat of his body to relax me.

"You need to get some rest," he said as he held me in his arms, stroking my hair.

"You too. I'm just happy you are here with me," I murmured into his chest.

"Same, baby, same."

A bit later, I rolled onto my opposite side and swallowed hard, trying to rid my throat of the large lump that sat in the centre of it. I'd just gotten comfortable when I felt Asher slide his arm under my neck and felt him press his body against my back, his other hand running around my waist, landing on my abdomen. On our baby. He kissed my neck.

"Good night, sweetheart," he whispered. In a matter of moments, I lay there fighting the burning sensation behind my eyes, while he drifted off into a deep sleep. Here he was planning our future, and I was hiding something from him that would surely end it.

ASHER HAD BEEN asleep for a couple of hours; I was still awake. I'd been getting that nauseous feeling again and knew it was only going to be a matter of time before I needed to be sick. I slipped out from under the covers, careful not to disturb him. The last thing I wanted was for him to get up with me and wonder what the problem was. I pulled the door shut and bolted to the bathroom.

I'd just taken a cloth and wet it down, patting my face, when I thought I'd heard a noise. I listened hard. Whatever it was I'd heard stopped. I hung the cloth up over the edge of the tub and made my way out to the kitchen to make a hot cup of tea.

Thoughts of telling Asher about the baby were still running through my mind. Actually, they'd gotten worse once I knew he wanted to take things further with me. I knew that nothing good would come from me holding on to this information. I should have immediately come clean, and I never should have agreed to the weekend with him. Yet, I wanted to be with him. It was almost as if he were a drug, and I was being pushed by an unseen force toward him. I let out a sigh and carried my tea into the living room, grabbing my cell phone as I went.

I needed to unload some pressure, and the one part of this weekend that was stressing me out the most was having dinner with Brielle and Sawyer. I knew she wanted what was best for me, yet I was afraid that she might spill the beans about me being pregnant.

I sat down on the couch, pulling the blanket that lay across the back of it over me. After grabbing my phone, I sent a message to Brielle to cancel dinner. There was no reason for us to have dinner tonight. As soon as I sent the text, my phone vibrated. I should have known she'd be up and getting ready for work now.

> BRIELLE: What do you mean you're cancelling?

> BELLA: Just what I said.

> BRIELLE: What happened?

I tapped my phone. I didn't want to tell her he'd spent the night. I also didn't want to tell her that a few moments ago I'd decided that after the weekend I was going to tell him I no longer wanted to see him. Yet, as if someone else had my phone, that was exactly what I'd typed.

> BRIELLE: WHAT? He's there now? Girl, you are in a pretty messed-up situation! What do you mean after this weekend you're going to break things off? What is going on in that head of yours? It's pregnancy hormones, isn't it?

> BELLA: Yes, it's a fucked-up situation. Yet, if you knew what I know, you'd do the same thing. So, let me have my weekend with him and let me say good-bye in my own way.

I dropped the phone beside me and placed my head in

my hands. I wanted to cry. Losing him was the last thing I wanted. I sat like that for a few minutes, until I heard the bedroom door open. I grabbed my mug and leaned back against the couch, curling my feet underneath me, pretending as if nothing were wrong.

"Morning." A very sexy, sleepy-looking Asher emerged from the hallway.

"Morning. Want a tea? The kettle should still be hot."

He made his way over to me and knelt in front of me, taking the mug from my hands. He looked into my eyes and smiled. "I have to get going. I have appointments this morning, but I'm looking forward to dinner tonight and spending time with you."

"Oh, about that. Brielle had to cancel. She isn't feeling well. Baby things." I shrugged.

"Oh, is that why you're up? Is she okay? Do you need to go in for her?"

"Yeah, unfortunately, I do. I told her we'd reschedule."

"Oh, okay. Well then, I guess I will pick you up tonight for our weekend."

I smiled, placed my hand on his cheek, and leaned forward, meeting his lips. "Can't wait."

Once he stood, I got up off the couch and followed him to the door. He turned and kissed me good-bye, then opened the door and took off down the hall.

I made my way back to the couch and grabbed my phone. There was a pile of missed messages.

BRIELLE: I wish you'd come to your senses

BRIELLE: It's not fair to him what you are doing

BRIELLE: It's not fair to yourself either

BRIELLE: You are so damn stubborn

BRIELLE: He isn't Miles! I wished you'd of kicked that asshat to the curb years ago! Just like I told you!

BRIELLE: My god! I can't believe you are just going to spend the weekend with him and get that much closer to him just to end things.

BRIELLE: For the love of god woman! Now you aren't answering me either.

BRIELLE: UGH!!!! You're impossible!

I thought for a moment. She was right. Everything she was saying was right! I blew out a breath, and then I responded to her.

BELLA: I know what I am doing. I am giving my heart a chance to say goodbye. I really like him and wish things were way different, but they aren't. I'll message you later.

I placed my phone down on the table and sat back with my tea. The instant it vibrated against the tabletop, I reached over and hit the power button. I needed time to digest what it was I was doing, and I didn't need to hear it from Brielle. I knew what I was doing was wrong, and I already felt guilty about it.

Bella

It was Saturday night. The weekend had seemed to fly by in a flash. We'd spent Friday night sharing a wonderful dinner in the moonlight in his backyard, followed by two movies that neither of us barely watched. This morning we got up, went for a yoga session, and then spent the day up the coast at the fall fair. Afterward, we made our way back to Eastport, stopping at a local bookstore for a coffee and some browsing. We returned to his place where we cooked dinner together.

Now we lay on our backs looking up at the night sky. We'd made our way down to the beach, where we'd spread out a big blanket, threw two pillows down, and once we were comfortable, he covered us with another blanket. We'd been out here for a couple of hours now, watching a meteor shower.

"Did you see that one?" I cried. "It was so bright."

"I did. Probably the best one of the night," he said, pulling me tighter against him. It was early October, and it was colder than usual. The wind had picked up, and I shivered a little.

"You cold?" he asked

"Hmm, maybe a little."

He tightened his arm around me. "Want to lie on my other side? I'll block some of the wind."

"Do you mind?"

He shook his head and held on to me as I straddled his lap. He gripped my hips, stopping me. "This is something I might like to try," he said, holding me there and smiling up at me.

I laughed as my cheeks heated. "Might be able to be arranged," I said, bending down and meeting his lips.

I pulled my other leg over him and lay down on the other side of him. He was right; it was warmer, and I snuggled against him as he pulled the blanket up around my neck. "That better?"

"Much," I whispered, breathing in his scent.

He rolled onto his side and met my eyes. I could feel the intensity of his stare. "What is it?" I questioned.

"Nothing. Just, I've really enjoyed our time together this weekend."

"Same here."

He met my lips and kissed me hard, just as another

gust of wind blew. I shivered as we parted, and Asher looked down at me. "Want to head back inside?"

I could tell from the look in his eyes that he had other things on his mind that he'd rather be doing, and that they'd best be done inside and not on a beach, so we gathered all the blankets and made our way back to the house.

In a matter of minutes of being inside, he grabbed me and carried me down the hall to his bedroom. Placing me gently on the edge of the bed, he pushed me back and stood over me. He leaned down and kissed me hard. Then he stared down at me as he undid the buttons of my shirt, opening them one by one. His eyes fell to my breasts when he opened the clasp of my bra and he leaned down, tenderly kissing them. I closed my eyes as his fingers grazed the skin of my stomach and stopped at the button on my jeans. He flicked the button open and slid his hand into my pants, running his fingers between my legs.

Just lying in his arms outside had turned me on, and I was slightly embarrassed by how wet I was. Yet Asher licked his lips as he slid my pants off my body. He parted my legs and buried his face between them. I wanted to tell him to stop, but he gripped the waist of my panties and ripped at the lacy side, pulling them off me, then buried his face between my legs. My fingers instantly gripped his hair as my head fell back.

The feeling of his tongue on me was so strong that I felt like I could let go. I bit my bottom lip to keep from screaming when he stopped. Opening my eyes, I wondered what was going on. I looked to see that he stood before me, looking down at me. He'd removed his shirt and pants, and he stood there with his hand over his hardened cock, straining against his boxers. I pushed myself up and went to move his hand, but he stopped me.

"Lay back. Just let me look at you," he said, gripping his cock.

A little self-conscious, I laid back on the bed and met his eyes.

"Fuck, you're beautiful," he gritted.

I lay back there waiting for him to join me. I kept my eyes on his hand. He noticed, and pulled himself out of his boxers and began stroking himself. "You like that?" he questioned.

"Very much," I whispered as I concentrated on his hand and watched what he liked.

"Touch yourself?" he whispered. "I want to watch."

I'd done nothing like this before, and my heart raced as I shyly placed my hand over my breast, the other moving down toward my centre.

"That's it." He groaned. "Run your fingers between your legs." His voice was strained as he told me what he wanted.

I opened my eyes and watched as he gripped his hard cock in his hand, stroking himself at a slow pace as I ran my fingers through my wet centre.

My fingers circled the small bundle of nerves, a small moan escaped my lips. Instantly, I felt the bed dip and his large hand gripped mine and placed it on his cock. He placed his hand where mine had been and continued circling the little bud. The more he continued, the hotter my body got, even more so than I already had been. His cock slid through my fingers and my thumb spread that small bead of pre-cum over the head. He groaned and slid one and then two fingers inside of me, gently fucking me.

He met my mouth while he pumped his fingers into me. Our lips parted. I continued stroking him while he pulled his fingers from me, leaving a void I wanted to have filled again. He pulled my hand away from his cock and quickly moved between my legs and gripped my hips, lining himself up at my entrance.

Our eyes locked as he slid into me, slowly inching his way in until he was buried deep inside of me. The void that had been begging to be filled was now content. He held himself there for a moment, deep inside of me, barely moving his hips, then began moving in slow, deep bursts. I'd felt nothing this good before.

As he continued, I closed my eyes and held his hands. I could feel the threat of my orgasm ready to come on already. I didn't want this to end. He must have sensed it because he stopped moving and pulled out of me, then slid himself right back in. He did this move a few times, stopping and kissing me before he slammed himself back into me.

"Oh God, Asher. Do that again...please," I begged.

"Come for me, Bella," he said, breathing heavily while repeating the same thing over and over. "Come hard."

He found the swollen little bud and began stroking his thumb over it as he pumped in and out of me, faster but just as deep.

I gripped the blankets and cried out as he continued stroking me. I clenched tightly around him, feeling my body let go.

"That's it, baby. Let go." He groaned as he continued thrusting deep and fast into me, until his body tensed and he let go, collapsing onto me.

We lay in bed wrapped in one another in the wee hours of Sunday morning. I was exhausted. We hadn't only had sex once but twice, and only a few minutes ago, the third time ended. Only something had changed. It was slower, more sensual, and when it was over, he'd pulled me into his arms and held me in a way he hadn't before. Everything from the way he'd looked at me, the way he'd touched me, to the way he'd kissed me had changed.

I lay with my eyes closed, feeling his light breath against my shoulder. He was wrapped around me in a protective embrace that I loved. I swallowed hard as I thought back to how things were even different from Thursday night. As the weekend passed, I'd noticed many little things had changed. Conversations flowed way easier between us, and all those accidental touches felt normal but still sent waves through me. Our hands lingered longer on each other, and we fell into sync with one another. Everything was different with Asher than it had ever been with Miles.

I was certain Asher was asleep, and I let out a ragged breath. Anxiety had filled me, and it felt like I had an elephant sitting on my chest just thinking about what tomorrow night would be like when I told him I couldn't do this anymore. I shifted my body a little, trying to get comfortable.

"What's wrong?" he whispered and pulled me tighter into him.

"Nothing. I... I just a bad dream," I replied, rubbing his muscular forearm. I wasn't lying. This entire situation was a nightmare.

"Can't have that," he whispered, his lips kissing my bare shoulder, up my neck to my ear. I rolled a little onto my back, where I met his mouth.

He kissed me slow, and as our lips parted, he met my eyes. "Can I tell you something?"

I nodded.

"I think I'm falling in love with you." He met my lips again, kissing me deeper, his tongue washing through my mouth.

I was screwed.

Bella

"Brie, I have to go to my doctor's appointment at one today," I said as Brielle walked into the office where I was working on the upcoming schedule.

"No problem. Will you be coming back afterward?"

"I dunno. What's this appointment like?" I asked, looking at her growing belly.

"Ah, let me think. It should just be an ultrasound. You should be fine. Did you want me to go with you? I mean, I could," she said, glancing around at the mess on her desk.

"No, I was just wondering."

"Well, it's totally up to you. See what time your appointment ends, and if you don't feel like coming back, then it's not a big deal. You were in early today anyway. I don't think we are going to be that busy tonight."

"Okay, thanks."

"I noticed Asher was here last night when I left."

"Yeah, he came by to see me. I hope it's okay that I took my dinner hour with him?"

Brie frowned. "I thought you were going to end things with him?"

She was right. I was supposed to end things with him three weeks ago. Only I hadn't been able to. Every single time I'd gathered the courage, I fell in love with him a little more. My heart was content and happy, something it hadn't been in years.

I shrugged. "I was, but..."

"But what?" Brie stood there looking at me, her hand on her hip, waiting for me to respond.

Suddenly, Sawyer appeared in the doorway. In one hand, he held what was surely Brie's lunch and her laptop bag.

"You forgot these in the car." He smiled, stepping in and placing them down on the floor beside the desk. I watched as he placed his hand on her belly, leaned in, and kissed her. "I'll pick you up after work, okay, baby? Take it easy today," he said, kissing her again before even noticing I was in the room.

"Hey, Bella. How you feeling?"

"Good, Sawyer, thanks for asking." I smiled, watching as he kissed her again.

"How's the morning sickness?"

"It's changed to mid-afternoon." I giggled, and Sawyer laughed, patting my shoulder before he left.

Brielle shifted a few things around on her desk, making room for her laptop.

"That's what I want."

"What?" Brie asked, looking at me over her shoulder.

"That. I want that. You and Sawyer have what I want. That is something I want with Asher. That's why I haven't told him yet. I mean, look at the two of you."

Brie sat down and slid her chair over to me. "If you want what we have, then you need to tell him. But know that things weren't always this way between us. It took a long while for him to trust me again. I mean, I robbed Sawyer of experiencing all the baby things with Emma. The only memories he has of her were from the time he met her to now. I was wrong about doing that. You're wrong to do this to him."

"I know."

"I just don't understand what the big deal is?"

"Brie, he told me he doesn't want children."

"When did he say that?"

"He told me back before I knew I was pregnant. Well, before I knew anyway. He thinks I can't have children, and he was relieved. He didn't even falter when I told him."

Brielle looked at me, her arms crossed over her chest. "Bella, I don't know what to tell you. You can't keep doing this to him, or yourself. You are going to end up hurt if you don't figure things out."

"I'd planned on doing it. I just... I couldn't."

"Why not?"

"Because I'm in love with him."

The room grew quiet. Brielle stood there looking at me, while I just wanted to crawl under the desk and hide.

"I don't know what to tell you. Just tell him soon or I can guarantee he's going to find out. Eventually, you're gonna pop, and...."

"I know...I know...I'll tell him this weekend. We are going to a music festival up the coast. When he drops me off on Sunday, I'll do it."

I sat in the waiting room reading a magazine that I'd found lying on the table. I glanced down at my watch. It was already half an hour past my appointment time. I frowned, wondering what was taking so long. I threw the magazine down and picked up another one when I heard my name called.

A nurse stood inside the door that led to the waiting room. I smiled, placed the magazine back on the table, and followed her down the hall. I followed her into an exam room, where I saw a gown on the end of the table.

"Sorry, Bella, Doctor Love had an emergency delivery,

which is taking longer than expected. He asked me to do your ultrasound. He's hoping by that time he'll be back up to finish your appointment."

"Oh, well, I can always come back another day if it's more convenient."

"Nope, no need. These things sometimes happen. We will get everything taken care of. So, please, get undressed. You may leave your undergarments on, gown open at the front. I'll be back in a few minutes." She smiled as she pulled the door closed, leaving me in the empty room.

I placed my things on the chair in the corner and began getting undressed. I was feeling nervous about this appointment, and I wished I'd taken Brielle up on her offer to come with me today. It would have helped to calm me down a little to have her here, I thought to myself.

Once I had the gown on, I pulled it closed at the front and hopped up onto the end of the table and sat there waiting. Finally, I heard a soft knock on the door and it opened an inch.

"Alright, Bella, all ready?" the nurse asked, taking a peek into the room. Once she saw me sitting there, she closed the door behind her. Then she pulled the curtain closed around the table.

She adjusted the table a bit. "Alright just lean back here," she said, standing beside me while I shifted myself and rested my back against the cold paper-covered table.

I watched as she walked around and turned on the

monitor, then she grabbed a tube of jelly. "This may be a little cold," she said, removing the sides of my gown off my belly and squirting some gel onto my skin.

"Oh God, doesn't this stuff come warmed up?" I said, giggling.

"I know. It's a shocker." She smiled. "Now just relax."

She sat down on the chair and grabbed a wand, rolling it over my abdomen. "You may be uncomfortable with the pressure, but this shouldn't take too long."

I watched as she rolled the wand around my abdomen while looking at the screen. After a few seconds, I began leaning forward, trying to see the screen. When she noticed, she smiled. "There isn't a lot to see right now," she said and turned the monitor a little toward me. "Do you have any other children?"

"No, this is my first," I said, still watching the screen for anything I might see.

"Ah, now I know why you're so keen on seeing what is going on." She studied the screen intently, moving the wand around a little, and then smiled. "And there you are," she quietly said.

"Where?"

She pointed to this little odd shape on the screen. "Right there."

I frowned. "That's it?"

"That's it!" She smiled. "Don't worry, most first-time

parents say the same thing. It's like a little kidney bean, isn't it?"

I nodded, still watching the screen. "That's what has been responsible for my morning sickness?"

"That's it! Amazing that something that tiny can do that to us, isn't it?"

I nodded, watching as she marked a few things down on the paper in front of her. Then she took a paper towel and cleaned the wand off and passed me a pile of them.

"Alright, my dear, once you get dressed, you can head through the side door into Doctor Love's office. I'm just going to get this image printed off and a report ready for him, and hopefully, fingers crossed, he should be here in about twenty minutes."

"Thank you," I said.

Once she was gone, I did as I was told, cleaning myself up, then getting dressed, and then I made my way into his office. I took a seat on the comfortable-looking couch in his office and pulled my phone from my pocket.

There was a message from Asher. I smiled as I read it.

ASHER: Will be a little late tonight picking you up. Work issues. I should be there by seven thirty. We'll get dinner to go, then head up to the hotel. ;)

BRIELLE: Sounds good, take your time ;)

Asher

I stood in line for a coffee in the hospital cafeteria when my phone vibrated in my pocket. Today of all days, one of Alonzo's patients had to go into labour. She'd had a high-risk pregnancy as it was, and both Alonzo and I had been glad he was here to deal with it. I'd seen her once during her second trimester, and she'd been a basket case, worried that Alonzo was going to abandon her. My phone vibrated again, and I pulled it out, looking at the screen.

BELLA: Sounds good, take your time ;)

I quickly sent another message.

ASHER: This is what my career is like. I hope you can take it

I watched as the three little dots bounced up and down.

> BELLA: I know, Brielle complains all the time about Sawyer, at least I can now relate :D

I let out a laugh.

> ASHER: Hope you don't complain about me.

> BELLA: Not yet, you've only made me wait twice. Although one more time that will give me rights to start lol

I smiled. God, I loved her.

> ASHER: You all ready for the weekend?

> BELLA: all packed and ready when you are.

> ASHER: Bags in the car. Good thing I packed last night.

> BELLA: Looking forward to it. See you tonight. Hope your day goes by fast.

I pocketed my phone just as I got to the counter. I

ordered my coffee and a muffin and headed back upstairs. It would have been nice to get out of the office for a bit and head to The Cooling Rack for lunch, but this would have to do. I'd just walked through the doors of the office. The waiting was room full. Marie waved, catching my attention. I shut the outside door and made my way over to her desk.

"Asher, Alonzo is stuck downstairs. Apparently, some complications arose, and he's had to do a C-section. I've rescheduled most of his appointments the second I found out. However, there is one patient here that is waiting for him in his office."

"Okay, no big deal. I can take care of it," I said, glancing down at my watch.

"It shouldn't take you long. It's an eight-week ultrasound. Everything is already done. You just need to go over the results."

"Sure, no problem. These are actually a favourite of mine. However, I'll need you to cancel my six o'clock then. Try to reschedule for Monday."

"Ah, yes, you have that festival this weekend, don't you?"

"Yep, and now I don't feel so bad asking Alonzo to watch over my three ladies who may go into labour this weekend, knowing he will probably be here anyway." I chuckled.

"That's okay. He'll get you back next weekend," Marie

said, smiling. "I'll get that appointment rescheduled. I can also reschedule your five thirty if you like."

I thought for a moment. "Please do. That will help a bit, just in case I run over with the rest of the appointments this afternoon."

I headed on down the hall, carrying my hot coffee into my office. I took a few sips, a couple bites of the sandwich I'd been working on for most of the afternoon, and then headed toward Alonzo's office, pulling the file out of the file hanger and opening it to glance and make sure the results were there. Sure enough, the page was on top, and I opened the office door.

"Hello, sorry about the wait. Doctor Love had an emergency and unfortunately can't make it. I'm Doctor Harrison and I'll..."

As I turned around, I stopped dead in my tracks as I laid eyes on my next patient. Bella stood in front of me, the look on her face matching mine. With our eyes locked, it was all I could do to stand there as shock flooded my body. Neither of us moved. In fact, I wasn't even sure if I was still breathing. My hands shook as I tilted the file to see the name of the patient, and sure enough, Bella Langdon was neatly typed on the nameplate.

The silence in the room was deafening. I could barely take it. I looked at her; she looked at me; I felt completely blindsided. "Is this some sort of joke?" I asked.

She didn't move; she just stood there.

"What kind of sick joke is this, Bella?" I asked again, raising my voice.

"It's not a joke," she whispered, her voice barely audible.

"You're here for an eight-week ultrasound? You're pregnant?"

She barely nodded her head, but she did, in fact, nod.

"I take it… fuck me… that it's mine, unless there are other things you aren't telling me?"

She nodded her head as her bottom lip trembled.

The room spun as I stood there. I needed to sit down, but that would mean I'd want to entertain a conversation with her and really all I wanted was to run from this room. Instead of responding, I turned and left. I shut the door behind me and made my way into my office where I took a seat. I just needed to breathe, I thought to myself as I studied the wall.

After I'd taken a few deep breaths, and once the room finally stopped spinning and I didn't feel as if I would faint away, I got up. Leaving the file on my desk, I made my way back toward Alonzo's office, opened the door, and slipped inside to find Bella sitting on the edge of the couch, her face in her hands.

"How long have you known?" I demanded, trying to keep my voice down.

She shrugged. "About six weeks."

"So you've known since before you came back to East-port?" I bit out as I paced back and forth.

She slowly nodded her head.

"So, was it all a lie?"

"What?"

"Was it all a lie? The 'I can't get pregnant' part. Was it all a lie?"

"What? No…"

"'Cause it seems to me that it might have been."

She let out a cry. "No, Asher, I wasn't lying," she said, standing up and taking a step toward me.

"Don't come near me," I spat as I listened to her sobs.

Bella stopped in her tracks, tears streaming down her face.

"Why didn't you just tell me?"

She looked at me, shifted from one foot to the other. "Because you told me you didn't want kids, that you hated them. Which honestly makes zero sense to me when you are a pediatrician."

"Whoa, who said I was a pediatrician? This is my office. Doctor Love is my employee. I'm an OB/GYN, Bella. What reason would there be for me to be here if I were a pediatrician?"

Bella shrugged. "I don't know. You could work with Doctor Love."

I ignored that statement. "Oh, and I don't hate kids."

"Then why don't you want them?"

I ran my hand over my face. "I never said I never wanted them. I said I didn't want them with the woman in my previous relationship. There were many, many things wrong with that entire situation. For starters, she constantly lied to me. Lied about little things and then about bigger things when the truth would have been sufficient. I can't even begin to tell you how many things were wrong with that relationship, and there appears to be just as many things wrong with this one."

"Asher...I..."

"You what? Not being able to get pregnant is what you lied about. Then you failed to tell me you were. How do I know anything that has gone on between us and said during our time together hasn't been one big lie?"

Bella stood there, tears rolling down her cheeks as she listened. Soon, loud, guttural sobs fell from her.

"Yeah, that's exactly it. I don't know what the truth is any more than you do."

"Asher, none of it was a lie," she cried.

"Yeah, whatever you say," I said, moving toward the door.

"It's not like you were completely honest with me either," Bella said.

"What do you mean by that?"

"You never told me you were an OB/GYN. You also never told me you were opening a practice right here in the hospital, either."

"No, I didn't. You are correct. However, I didn't really think that my specialty really mattered all that much. It wasn't like I would not tell you either. When I wanted to tell you about this office, your mother got sick. You had to leave, but I did eventually tell you. Perhaps not when I should have, but I told you. If you wanted to know my specialty, all you needed to do was ask. It's not a state secret."

"You're no different from me."

Anger flooded through me. She was trying to place me on the same horse she was on. There was no way she was going to do that to me. I grabbed the handle of the door and pulled it open, ready to walk out and close the door on this part of my life. It was going to kill me to do it, but I'd do it.

"Asher... please wait..."

I stopped. My heart was racing when I turned around to face her. "Bella, I loved you. I allowed myself to open my heart once again, and as stupid as it was, I fell in love with you. Everything we had, all of this has been shot to hell now, don't you think?"

"No, we can work through this," she cried.

"I can't. I don't think I can trust you. I'm sorry." I said nothing more. I just stood there, staring at her, watching her cry. Then I shook my head. "It's over. I hope you enjoy your weekend. I sure as hell know I won't be enjoying mine."

I ripped the door open and pulled it shut behind me and went into my office. The patients could wait. I needed a minute. I needed an hour. Hell, I needed a long fucking time to get over this. I shut the door and leaned up against the wall, focusing on calming myself down. I didn't care how long she stayed in there. I just couldn't be there with her any longer. I walked over and sunk into my office chair, turning my attention to my next patient file. I had to get through the rest of my day, and the only way I was going to do it was to focus on my next task.

Bella

MY EYES PUFFY, my cheeks still tear-stained, I pulled a tissue from the box on Doctor Love's desk. Asher's words had torn my heart out. I'd been sitting here for twenty minutes, shocked to the core. I still wasn't sure what I'd been expecting him to say. I blew my nose, then grabbed two more tissues from the box that sat on Doctor Love's desk and dabbed my eyes. I needed to get out of this office.

I picked up my purse and walked to the door. The last thing I wanted was to run into Asher in the hallway. I took in a breath and pulled the door open enough to look out into the hallway. I glanced across the hall. The nameplate on the door read Asher Harrison. The door was tightly closed. I looked down the hall. The door to the waiting area seemed far away, yet this was probably my only chance.

I took off down the hall to the waiting room, and when I opened the door and stepped out of the hallway, everyone's eyes turned to me. They all stared. I was sure I was a sight with my puffy eyes and tear-stained face. Regardless, I gathered the courage and stepped into the room and headed for the door.

"Bella, before you go, we should book your next appointment in," the nurse behind the desk called out without looking up.

I swallowed hard. I turned my back toward her. "I'll call," I mumbled and stumbled out the door into the hallway of the thirteenth floor. I hit the button for the elevator and stood there, my vision blurring with fresh tears as memories from only a few minutes ago flooded my mind. Then I heard two voices and glanced down the hall to see Doctor Love rounding the corner with a nurse. I didn't want him to see me like this. It would lead to too many questions, ones I didn't want to answer right now. Instead of waiting for the elevator, I took off heading to the stairwell.

It took forever for me to walk down all those stairs and get outside to my car. Once I was seated behind the wheel, the tears flowed. I sat there sobbing into my hands. The look on his face sat in the forefront of my mind. Then his words—his harsh words—came into my head. Everything was a mess, and I had myself, and only myself, to thank for it.

My phone lay on centre console of the car, right where I'd thrown it, and there it vibrated. I glanced at it to see a message from Brielle. She was probably wondering where I was. I picked up the phone without reading it and turned it off, throwing it into my purse. I just wanted to be left alone.

Six hours later, I lay on my couch, wrapped in a blanket, absolutely exhausted from the events that had transpired through today. I stared at the television, barely hearing anything that was being said. I hadn't eaten; I wasn't hungry, and yet my stomach grumbled, telling me it wanted food.

I sat up and headed to the kitchen. After putting the kettle on, I put two pieces of bread in the toaster. I was supposed to have left with Asher for the weekend hours ago. He'd probably gone anyway, I thought to myself as I filled my mug with hot water and buttered my toast.

I woke early the next morning, my head still pounding, and jumped into the shower. I was exhausted, and my body ached from a terrible night's sleep. I'd finally turned my phone on before bed, hoping for a message from Asher, and each time I'd woken during the night, I'd checked to find nothing.

I'd gotten dressed and headed to the kitchen. I opened the fridge to get an apple, only to find out it was empty. Since I knew we were going away this weekend, I didn't do my regular grocery shop on Thursday. I let out a sigh. I'd have to get groceries. As much as I didn't want to leave, I figured that the fresh air would be good for me. I slipped my shoes on and grabbed my purse and keys.

I'd gotten the few things I needed from the store and then made my way over to The Cooling Rack. The fresh air had done me good, and now I needed my best friend. The parking lot was busy, but I found a spot. When I walked through the door, I could see from the look on her face that she was shocked to find me here after I took the weekend off to go away with Asher. I didn't need to say anything; she took one look at me and immediately wrapped me in her arms and directed me to this table where I currently sat.

She'd gone back to the counter and said something to the new hire behind the counter. Then she made her way over to the table carrying two blueberry muffins.

"They are bringing over two teas. I got you chamomile," she said, sliding the muffin in front of me.

"Thank you," I mumbled, breaking apart the muffin and taking a bite.

"We can go into the office if you'd prefer. More private. It's pretty busy here today," she said, glancing around at the full tables and the line of doctors that waited at the counter.

I shook my head. "No, it's fine. Hopefully, being in front of people will keep me from crying." I sadly smiled. "You were right. I should have told him," I muttered.

"What happened?" she questioned.

I took a minute and then looked at her with tears in my eyes. "It was awful. I went for my appointment with Doctor Love and, well, he had an emergency to tend to. I guess they passed me off to the next doctor, who was Asher."

Brielle's eyes shot up from her muffin and landed on mine. "What? When did this happen?"

Ignoring her question, I blurted, "He found out because I was standing in front of him waiting for my ultrasound results. I wanted to die."

"Oh, Bella." Brielle went to get up and move over beside me, but I stopped her.

"You'll make me cry..." I said, holding my hands out in front of myself. "It was awful. *He*, was awful."

"What did he say?"

My lip trembled, and I took a sip of tea to try and stop it. "He wanted to know why I just didn't tell him."

"And did you?"

I nodded. "Only he got angrier. It wasn't that he didn't want children at all. It was... that he didn't want them with her."

Brielle sat there waiting for me to continue, but when I didn't, she leaned forward. "I see it's rather a good mess you've gotten into isn't it."

I nodded, picking up my mug again. I took a sip and then told her the entire story, and how things had been left: with me standing alone in the office crying my eyes out. When I finished, she sat there, tears in her eyes as she studied me.

"What am I going to do?" I questioned.

"I don't know. Perhaps give it a few days, then try to talk to him," she suggested. "Sometimes, in the heat of the moment, people say things they don't mean. I mean, think about how you might feel if the shoe were on the other foot?"

I looked over at my best friend. *That was her advice! Give him a few days? Think about how I'd feel if the shoe were on the other foot.*

"Brielle, seriously."

"Yes, seriously. You've jumped to conclusions this entire time, you've lied to him—well, maybe not lied, but told untruths."

"That's what he said," I muttered.

"So, give him a few days."

"My God, that is the most awful advice anyone has ever given me."

"Why?"

"What do you mean, why? He said I was a liar, that everything we had was based on a lie. Do you really think he'd entertain a conversation with me?"

"I don't know, he might. If he's the man I think he is, he will. But I know for the sake of that baby, you need to try."

Asher

I'D BURIED myself in work since Friday. Finding out that Bella was pregnant had shocked me. Work had been the only way to escape the way I felt. I'd been blindsided. I was angry, and I'd acted out of that shock and anger. I'd been so mad I'd jumped to a conclusion that hadn't made me feel any better, despite thinking that was what I wanted. On top of all that, I was hurt. Over the course of our relationship, I'd always told her she could come to me with anything.

I'd worked the rest of that day on Friday and then left the office. I'd gone home and sulked around the house for the better part of Friday night and Saturday, but I needed to pull myself out of the funk I was in. I couldn't possibly see patients on Monday in this mood.

I'd sat down behind my desk with a hot cup of coffee

and switched my little radio on. I grabbed the file that lay on my desk for my first patient on Monday, looking over her test results, and made some notes to discuss some things with her. Then I moved onto the next. As I placed the last file Marie had left for me, I noticed one last file sitting on my desk. Bella's name stared me in the face.

I set it off to the side, but curiosity got the best of me. I flipped the file open and while I knew it was wrong to look over Alonzo's patient files, I did it anyways. I went right back to the beginning, looking over past blood work and diagnosis. She hadn't been lying; Kavanaugh had diagnosed her as infertile. The old bastard hadn't even done his due diligence and ran the proper tests. It didn't come as a shock to me. I'd found it in some of my own patient files.

I continued, flipping through notes from her appointment with Alonzo, and then to her blood work results. I ran my hand over my face and then flipped to the ultrasound image. I stared at that little bean, while in my head I replayed the entire event over and over in my mind, realizing that my reaction to the situation was just as bad, if not worse than her not telling me. She was probably afraid to say anything to me after what I'd told her. She was probably shocked to find out that what she'd come to believe over the past five years hadn't been true.

Bottom line was, I'd been a complete dick. I flipped the report over and saw that the baby, our baby... my baby, would be born somewhere within the first two weeks of June. I flipped her file closed and leaned back in my chair. I'd royally fucked up. I picked up my phone. Tapping the side, I opened a new message to Bella, then decided against it. She deserved an apology, face-to-face, not a fucking text message.

When I climbed into my car, I checked the time. It was a little after five. Bella normally closed The Cooling Rack tonight. I decided I'd go there first. As I made my way there, I played in my mind what it was I'd say to her.

I'd start by apologizing and take it from there. Only when I pulled into the parking lot, I didn't see her car. Regardless, I cut the engine and headed inside to find Brielle standing behind the counter dealing with a customer. The look on her face said everything I needed to know. She knew.

I waited, and once she was done, she turned her back on me and began filling the counter.

"Brielle, is Bella here?" I asked.

She ignored me, continuing to fill the counter.

"Brielle?"

She popped her head up to the top of the counter and glared at me. "No, Asher, she isn't here."

"Do you know where she is?"

She laughed. "You think I'm going to tell you after what happened?"

I shrugged, hoping she would.

"If you think I am, you're wrong. She is fucking heartbroken. One bastard in her life was enough. I will not stand by and watch another one treat her the same way."

"Look, not that I need to explain myself to you, but I think you're being a little harsh, don't you?"

"Not really."

I gave up and turned and headed for the door. "If you won't tell me where she is, I'll find her on my own," I said as I stopped at the door.

I made my way back to my car and climbed in. I wasn't giving up. I looked up the number for the local florist and ordered two dozen white roses, then headed off to pick them up.

With flowers in hand, I took the elevator to her floor and walked down the hall. I stopped to catch my breath and then knocked on the door. When she didn't answer, I knocked again, this time calling her name. Still no answer. I felt my phone vibrate in my pocket and switched the flowers to the other arm, while pulling my phone out to see it was the hospital. One of my patients had gone into labour and was on the way. "Fuck," I muttered, shoving my phone back into my pocket.

I knocked one more time, harder, and called her name a little louder. Again nothing. There was nothing I could do. I had to go. I placed the vase on the floor outside of her door and took off down the hall, making my way back to the hospital.

I ended up at the hospital for the better part of the night. Just as I was leaving, one of Doctor Love's patients came in. A young single mother had gone into labour. She was scared and alone and became even more afraid when I notified her I was the OB/GYN on call for the weekend. I'd spent some time with her, calming her down. When I asked about the father, she told me he wanted nothing to do with her. She admitted she was terrified to be facing all of this alone. People said I had a great bedside manner, that I knew exactly what to say, but Alonzo was the one who was perfect with these situations. I silently cursed him for not being here while I tried to say something to comfort her.

I went through the motions that night, while listening to her cries. Her words had ripped at my heart, because all I kept thinking about was Bella. She felt the same way as this young girl did—scared, alone and unsupported. I imagined this being Bella's situation, and that was the last thing I wanted for her. Hell, I didn't want this for anyone.

Before I left the hospital, I popped in to check on her. She lay there, holding her baby, whispering to her. I smiled. "How are we doing?" I asked, checking over her chart.

"Okay. Tired."

"Did you decide on a name?" I questioned.

"I think I'm going to call him Asher." She smiled,

looking down at her baby. "I want to be reminded of how much you helped me tonight."

"Well, it's my job." I winked. "I've delivered lots of babies."

"Not for that. For your words, your kindness and your patience. Also, for not judging me."

I placed her file back in the holder at the bottom of her bed and nodded. "Good luck. Doctor Love will check in with you next week. Get some rest."

I stood there as she went back to talking to her baby and I walked to the door. I paused just before opening the door and turned back. "Oh, Crystal."

"Yeah."

"Thank you."

"For?" she asked, looking at me.

"For helping me." I pulled the door open and walked out into the hall. Taking my jacket off, I headed toward the parking lot.

Bella

I WENT to step out into the hall to head to my yoga class and almost tripped on the vase of white roses that sat just outside my door. I looked up and down the hall expecting to see the person who'd dropped them there, but there was no one. I looked back down to the flowers then bent down and picked them up.

I carried them into the kitchen and placed them on the counter. They were stunning, I thought to myself and leaned in and placed my nose on top of one rose, inhaling. Then I noticed the white card stuck inside, my name written on the small envelope. I pulled the envelope out of the flowers and opened it, removing the small card from inside.

The only thing written on the card was Asher's name. The other side of the card was blank as I flipped it over. I softly smiled. This was exactly him, but if he thought flowers were going to fix this, he was wrong. I shoved the card in the small envelope and threw it down on the counter.

I headed to the door, grabbing my mat and small bag on the way. I looked back at the roses, thinking about calling Asher but decided against it. I had a yoga class to get to.

The music played on as the class went into a few moments of silence. I lay on my mat at the end of class, in a corpse pose with my eyes closed, inhaling and exhaling as guided by the yogi. For the first time, I'd done exactly as instructed and could bring my mind to a clear state, letting go of everything.

"Now, slowly sit up and come into easy pose, bringing your hands to your heart's centre. Everything I need is within my reach. I am exactly where I am supposed to be," she said quietly. "The light in me honors the divine and beautiful light in each one of you. I wish you peace, love, and light, and may the rest of your week be as beautiful as you are. Thank you for joining me today."

The rest of the class began gathering their things, but I lay back on my mat again, just soaking in all the calmness I felt here. Yoga was exactly what I needed, I thought to myself. When the last person left the room, I rolled into a sitting position and began gathering my things, shoving them into my bag.

On my way home, I stopped at the grocery store and made my way over to the produce section. I shoved three apples and two oranges into a bag and threw them into my grocery basket, moving on over to the salads. I placed my basket on the floor between my feet and had just picked up two pre-made salads, trying to decide between them, when I heard a familiar voice.

"You'll like the one in your left hand better."

I spun to see Asher standing there holding a basket full of produce. He smiled. "How you doing?" he questioned.

"I've been better." I shrugged, turning my attention back to the salads in my hand.

"If you choose the one in your right hand, you'll have to pick out all the sliced olives," he said, stepping closer. My body immediately responded to the warmth his body was giving off.

I nodded and placed the other salad into my basket before putting the other back.

"Did you get my flowers?" he questioned.

"I did, but, Asher, flowers aren't going to fix this," I said quietly, fighting back tears as the memory of what he'd said came flooding back.

"I know that. I didn't think they would. You were supposed to be home when I brought them to you."

I had been home. I'd put my headphones in and hid in my bedroom, because when I'd heard his voice at the door,

I knew I wasn't ready to face him. I'd have crumbled, and that was something I had promised not only myself but Brielle I wouldn't do.

He bent down and picked my basket up off the floor. Then he leaned into me and whispered, "Meet me in your car. I'll take care of these."

His breath tickled my neck, chills running through my body, and the scent of his cologne was enough to drive me mad. I nodded and turned, leaving the grocery store. No matter how much I wanted to push him away, I couldn't. One look in his eyes was all it took.

As I walked to the car, I thought about the other two times I'd seen him this week. First out for a run Sunday morning in the park, then at The Cooling Rack when Brielle ripped him a new ass, which right after that I'd rushed home after seeing the pain in his eyes. I'd spent that night in tears, and now today.

I had been in the car about five minutes when Asher appeared, walking across the parking lot and opening my back door. He placed the bags in the back seat and climbed into the front passenger's seat. He'd barely gotten the door closed when I turned to him.

"I swear to you, I didn't lie about anything. It was all true. I was just afraid that if you found out you'd push me away."

"I know," he said.

"I swear, the diagnosis was real. I spent the last five years of my life living with that diagnosis over my head."

"I know."

"You aren't the only one in shock here, you know. I had finally accepted it and had moved on. Then you happened, and now...this."

"I know it all."

I'd finally stopped for a moment and heard what Asher had said for the third time. I looked at him, while the words sunk into my head. "You know?" I questioned.

"I know. I know it all. After you left, I continued with my day. It was the only thing I could do. I had patients waiting. I also didn't want to accept what it was I'd just found out. When I got home, the full magnitude of what had happened sent me into spiral I couldn't control. I spent the night moping around the house, Saturday as well. When Sunday came, I left for my morning run and headed to the office to get my head back in the game. I literally let go of my last career, virtually giving up. I wasn't about to do that with this one. As I was going through patient files, focusing on my upcoming week, I found yours."

"And..."

"Don't kill me. I shouldn't have done it, I know, but I read it."

"I see."

"I quickly learned that Kavanaugh had diagnosed you

as you said, but I also noticed his lack of testing. He'd not only done it to you, but I've found things in other client files that weren't necessarily done correctly. Anyway, I read through it all, and I did it with a lump in my throat and pain in my chest as my heart crumbled once again into a million pieces. I'd made assumptions based on anger and shock. I want you to know I was wrong in doing that."

"Yes, you were."

Asher took a minute. "I was also wrong to treat you the way I did. I was shocked and upset that you didn't feel comfortable enough to come to me. Most of all, as I read through everything, I realized what I'd thrown away was something I wanted, and I wanted it more than anything in my life."

"What's that?" I questioned.

Asher looked down at his hands, then looked back up at me and met my eyes. "You."

A tear slid down my cheek, and I wanted to kick myself for allowing it to happen while he was sitting right here. I was supposed to be being strong, and instead I was unraveling.

"I wanted you, and everything that comes along with you, Bella. If I'd only taken a minute to step back, take a breath, and approach this with some form of rationale then we wouldn't be in this position." He swallowed hard. "I'm so fucking sorry I hurt you, and while I can't take back what's been done, I can go forward and prove to you

I'm a much better man than that," he finished, his voice shaking.

Our eyes locked. I wanted to be in his arms so bad it hurt. Tears rolled down my cheeks. I hadn't wanted to cry in front of him, and yet here I was, sitting in my car, in a grocery store parking lot, a sobbing, crying mess.

He reached over and cupped my cheek, wiping the tears away. "Shall we try again?"

Asher

I opened my locker and pulled out a clean pair of scrubs. I stripped off the dirty ones and threw them into the hamper at the end of the aisle. I glanced to the clock on the wall. It was almost two. I threw on the pants and reached into my jeans pocket, pulling out my phone. Sure enough, I had two missed messages.

> BELLA: I'm here.

> BELLA: I hope you're going to make the appointment in time.

I threw my shirt over my head, locked my locker, and rushed out of the change room heading toward the elevator. The second I'd hit the button, I messaged her.

ASHER: On my way.

Bella and I had worked every single day on our relationship over the past six weeks. She even admitted to me after we'd gotten back together that she'd asked Sawyer to set her up with a psychologist to work through the trauma her ex had caused. I could tell she'd been nervous when she told me, but I listened with patience and understanding, letting her know that there was nothing wrong with that. I'd even attended a couple of her sessions with her.

The door to my office waiting room was open, and I saw Bella sitting in the corner. She waved and placed the magazine she'd been reading down. I walked over and sat down beside her, kissing her cheek. "How you doing?"

"Okay." She smiled, taking hold of my hand. "How was your morning?"

"Crazy busy. I almost didn't think I was going to get here in time," I said. "I even put on clean scrubs for the occasion." I winked at her.

Bella laughed. "I'm kind of glad you did. It may traumatize me seeing you covered in all the... Oh God, just the thought of it is going to make me sick," she said, sitting forward and covering her mouth.

"Just breathe," I said, rubbing her back.

A few moments later, we made our way down the hall to one of the exam rooms. I waited outside while Bella changed, and when she called to me, I stepped inside. She sat at the end of the table, her socked feet dangling as she held her gown closed. I walked over to her and kissed the side of her neck.

"None of that now."

"None of what?"

"Patient/doctor shenanigans." She giggled.

I laughed. "In order for that, you'd have to be my patient. You chose my colleague." I tsked.

A knock on the door caused us both to jump a little, and in walked Alonzo. "Hey, guys," he said, washing his hands in the small sink. "How are we today?"

"A little tired," Asher said.

Alonzo looked at Bella and then at me. "Asher, I meant Bella."

The three of us laughed.

"I'm good. Feeling good," she said.

"Well then, let's get to it, shall we?" Alonzo took a seat beside the table, while I adjusted the back of the table and guided Bella to lie back. Alonzo squirted some of the jelly onto Bella's barely-there baby bump.

"God, I hate that part. It's so cold," she said, taking my hand.

I placed one elbow on the back of the table and stood

beside her, my hand over hers, as I watched the screen as Alonzo moved the wand around. Then he stopped. "Before I continue, I just want to make sure you both want to know what the sex is."

Bella looked up at me, and I to her, both of us saying yes at the same time.

"Okay, just wanted to be certain. I know one of you knows how to read these." He chuckled. "Wanted to make sure it was going to be fair to everyone," he said, winking at Bella.

I felt her grip on my hand as he moved the wand around a little more, no doubt applying a little pressure. "Okay, well, everything is looking good. I am almost certain that it's a girl."

Bella looked up at me, her eyes shining with tears. I leaned down and kissed her forehead while Alonzo passed her a small towel.

"I'm just going to give you guys a few moments," he said, quietly getting up from the stool and leaving the room.

"Are you happy?" Bella asked once the door was closed.

I smiled at her, nodded my head, bent down, and met her lips. "Very," I whispered. "What about you?"

"Very... and nervous."

"No need to be. I'm here," I said, wrapping my arms around her. "I'm not going anywhere. I'm here."

Want more Asher and Bella?
GRAB THE BONUS SCENE

To get your FREE bonus scene visit
https://geni.us/DoctorRightBonusScene

Doctors of Eastport General

I hope you enjoyed my book, Doctor Right, which is part of the shared world Doctors of Eastport General.

Would you like to read all of them? Find them here on Kindle Unlimited.

Come on in and meet the new ER Physicians, Surgeons, Specialists, Residents, and patients that occupy the rooms and halls of the largest hospital on the coast of Rhode Island. You may even run into some of the doctors from Season 1. We hope you are ready to fall in love with all the new sexy stories that take place inside the walls of Eastport General Hospital.

Doctor Irresistible – Syd Ryan
Doctor Mistake – Amy Stephens
Doctor Divine – Tracy Broemmer
Doctor, Please – Celeste Granger
Doctor Frank Enstein – CA King
Doctor Change of Heart – Amber Ghe
Doctor Rescue – Mel Walker
Doctor Delectable – TL Mayhew
Doctor Love – Adryan Hart
Doctor Danger – Pandora Snow
Doctor Stuck-Up – A.N. Waugh
Doctor Sinful – E.M. Shue
Doctor Right – S.L. Sterling

Titles from Season 1

Doctor Heartbreak by D.M. Davis
Doctor Feelgood by Amy Stephens
Doctor D's Orderly Affair by CA King
Doctor Trouble by E.M. Shue
Doctor Temptation by Syd Ryan
Dueling Doctors by DC Renee
Doctor Sexy by TL Mayhew
Doctor Fix-It by Mel Walker
Doctor One of a Kind by Anjelica Grace
Doctor Casanova by Emma Nichole

Dirty Doctor by Amanda Richardson
Doctor All Nighter by Adora Crooks
Doctor Desire by S.L. Sterling

What is coming next from S.L. Sterling

The Spencer Brooks Diaries
Our Little Wedding

Willow Valley
Letters from the Heart

About S.L. Sterling

USA Today Bestselling Author S.L. Sterling was born and raised in southern Ontario. She now lives in Northern Ontario Canada and is married to her best friend and soul mate and their two dogs.

An avid reader all her life, S.L. Sterling dreamt of becoming an author. She decided to give writing a try after one of her favorite authors launched a course on how to write your novel. This course gave her the push she needed to put pen to paper and her debut novel "It Was Always You" was born.

When S.L. Sterling isn't writing or plotting her next novel she can be found curled up with a cup of coffee, blanket and the newest romance novel from one of her favorite authors.

In her spare time, she enjoys camping, hiking, sunny destinations, spending quality time with family and friends and of course reading.

Join my Reader Group
Sterlings Silver Sapphires

Want to stay up to date
Sign up for my Newsletter

Visit my website

Other Titles by S.L. Sterling

It Was Always You

On A Silent Night

Bad Company

Back to You this Christmas

Fireside Love

Holiday Wishes

Saviour Boy

The Boy Under the Gazebo

The Greatest Gift

Into the Sunset

The Spencer Brooks Diaries

Our Little Secret

Our Little Surprise

The Malone Brother Series

A Kiss Beneath the Stars

In Your Arms

His to Hold

Finding Forever with You

Vegas MMA

Dagger

Doctors of Eastport General

Doctor Desire

Doctor Right

All I Want for Christmas (Contemporary Romance Holiday Collection)

Constraint (KB Worlds: Everyday Heroes)

Willow Valley

Memories of the Past

The Holiday Dilemma